THE

RELUCTANT

DECLINE OF

BILL PRICE

By David T. Snyder

Kleenan Press

Post Office Box 1213

Walled Lake, Michigan 48390-1213

Library of Congress Control Number 2008903606

Printed in the United States of America

ISBN 978-0-9745081-4-6

This book is dedicated

to those intrepid readers

who read the first two books

in the Bill Price Trilogy.

Chapter One

The old man – unsupported by the stout cane he firmly gripped near the bottom end – seemed like an easy mark to the two young thugs who approached him one evening outside The Bristol Bar and Grill. Wearing a dark suit with lapels that revealed its vintage, Bill Price had finished two vodkas and an early dinner in an establishment he had patronized for more than 30 years and was waiting with uncharacteristic patience the arrival of a friend and his car for a ride home. One of the young men noticed Price's thinning white hair and the cane, which he took as evidence of physical decline. His companion reached the same conclusion on the grounds of no evidence at all.

"Hey, Pops," the taller of the two said to Price as they drew within a few feet of him. He had pulled a switchblade knife from his pants pocket and brandished it in a threatening manner. "Let's see your wallet."

"Yeah," the other one added only a split second before the heavy handle of the old man's cane caught the knife-wielder broadly across the face, smashing his nose flat and breaking a variety of small bones and blood vessels. He dropped instantly and unconsciously to the ground, his knife skittering across the sidewalk as Price slammed his cane into the other man's knees. He, too, fell, still conscious but writhing in pain.

"You were saying?" Price inquired rhetorically before he reentered the restaurant to call the very police department that had employed him as a detective before his retirement more than a decade earlier.

Jack McCurdy, who had gone to retrieve the car while his long-time friend waited for him, pulled up to the curb outside The Bristol only minutes before the arrival of a police squad car and an emergency medical truck. The two young men were still laid out on the sidewalk, one silently and the other moaning like a soft wind blowing down a deserted corridor.

"Jesus," McCurdy exclaimed as Price emerged from the restaurant and walked over to the car. "What's up?" The answer barely surprised him, knowing, as he did, that his friend had been a magnet for trouble most of his long life, and had generally settled disputes with the directness apparent on the nearby sidewalk. "These guys are a couple of the lucky ones," he thought, observing the miserable spectacle. "They're still alive." He got out of the car and was discussing the situation with Price when the police and medical team arrived to collect his statement and the human debris, which took relatively little time once the two older men had been identified as retired police officers. McCurdy had once been a colleague of Price's on the metropolitan force but had spent his final working years as a detective with an outlying suburban department. He had been forced to take work in the suburbs by a rare conflict of policies in which the city department required local residency of their officers and his wife, Missy, insisted on a heavily mortgaged house away from traffic, other forms of congestion and major crime. McCurdy was tough enough in many ways, but had always been a poor match where Missy was concerned.

"I was wondering why you bought that cane," McCurdy said as they drove away from The Bristol bound for the high-rise apartment where Price had lived for several years since the death of Diana Hornbeck, the woman who had occupied his life for more than a quarter century.

"I've always wanted one, but it seemed a little phony when I was younger," Price replied. "At the time, I didn't realize its many uses." Actually, he had fully anticipated its uses, which explained the steel rod that had been installed for him into the core of the instrument. A cabinetmaker friend of Price's had done the work only a few months earlier. The retired detective, who only carried the cane occasionally and mainly for amusement, still toted his police pistol in a belt holster, but no longer wore the small backup ankle piece that had saved his life on at least one occasion.

"How about a nightcap?" McCurdy inquired, fully aware there would be a negative reply. With rare exception, Price now limited himself to two drinks and McCurdy had watched him fill that quota before dinner.

"I've got work to do," Price said, thinking mainly of a detailed model of Lord Nelson's flagship, Victory, a project that had occupied his recreational attention for more years than he cared to remember. He was now constructing a fourth version of the famous ship – each one a little larger and more exquisite than the last – which had carried the great British admiral to his death at Cape Trafalgar in 1805. Among Price's few close friends, there was the presumption he would build still another and more elaborate one should his faculties and manual capacities endure. One of them had suggested he was working his way up to the real thing, and all were impressed to varying degrees with the artistry he had achieved over the years.

"You'd rather work on that toy boat than have a drink with me," McCurdy said, knowing his friend's habits as well as he knew his own.

"It's a ship, you moron," Price replied to a man who knew a boat from a ship. McCurdy had done service in the U.S. Navy in his late teens, just as Price had been in the Marine Corps about the same time. They had also sailed Price's 19 foot Lightning Class boat for many years at the Lake Millstone Yacht and Tennis Club, a modest accumulation of small vessels named in humor by its founding members with the full knowledge there would likely never be a tennis court on its small premises. There was, however, a clubhouse and bar that resembled a run-down roadhouse where domestic beer and a variety of jerky were the staples.

The two men lapsed into silence for most of the drive to Price's apartment, lost in thoughts they would have been hard pressed to define. Although they had met with great frequency over the years – mostly as friends but also as colleagues in several prolonged police investigations - they often went for long wordless periods together. Neither of them was particularly talkative, especially about small matters, and their individual interests outside police work were quite different. They had, in fact, little in common apart from their taciturn natures and work history, but for some inexplicable reason were mutually tolerant of each other's peculiarities.

There was among veterans of the city police force the strong suspicion that Price on several occasions had taken liberties with the modern concept of justice. Some thought he had beaten to death a homicidal vagrant that had murdered the aunt who took him in as a teenager when his parents were killed in an automobile accident. He was also suspected of shooting to death a local mobster who had tried to kill him. There were other similar suspicions, all unproven, which McCurdy, knowing his friend, generally accepted as fact and gave his approval on the grounds of justifiable homicide. He saw Price as an honorable man with little tolerance on occasion for the cumbersome machinery of democratic government.

Jack McCurdy was a seasoned investigator who had conducted his professional life with consistent competence and done quite the opposite with personal and financial matters. Price – whose resources were quite substantial for a policeman as the result of prudent investments over time and an inheritance from his aunt – had bailed him out of debt on several occasions but could do little to repair his domestic troubles. Beginning in early middle age, McCurdy blundered into one infidelity after another and was never clever enough to disguise these indiscretions from his wife, who finally decided to match him affair for affair because she knew he couldn't afford a divorce. Despite a more than bumpy relationship, the two remained married, partially for financial reasons and partially for their five children but mostly because they were fond of each other.

Price had long since learned to accept his friend's deficiencies, assuming the faults were built in and there was little he could do about it. To his gradual surprise, however, the onset of age seemed to improve McCurdy's ability to manage money and his sexual impulses as well. It finally occurred to Price that his friend's children, now grown, were no longer a drain on his modest income, and that the other problem had simply diminished with time. He still had his horny moments, Price knew, but at greatly dispersed intervals and only when there was substantial stimulation from some mature woman who had not yet given up on the concept of romance.

"I have certain requirements of a woman these days," McCurdy had told Price earlier that evening at dinner. "They must appreciate wrinkles and it helps if they have impaired vision. If I'm in a supermarket and see a mature lady bumping into the produce counter or anything else, I go over and start a conversation." Price understood the joke but suspected there was more truth involved than McCurdy realized.

Less than a block from Price's apartment, McCurdy had stopped his car at a traffic signal, unaware another vehicle had pulled up behind him. Not in any particular rush, he was prepared to drive away when the light turned green, but didn't do it fast enough to suit the driver of the other automobile. That was apparent in a series of insistent horn blasts accompanied by particularly gross obscenities the driver, his head partially out the side window, screamed into the previously still night air. He was soon joined by others in the car, and it was apparent to both McCurdy and Price that their antagonists were quite drunk and probably young.

The two retired policemen looked at one another, partly amused and partly annoyed, and wordlessly got out of their car and approached what turned out to be a reasonably new BMW from two sides. "Rich little bastards," McCurdy thought as he confronted the driver, who with his three friends were confounded by these aggressive old men in suits. One of them also noticed that Price had hooked a thumb in his belt, revealing the holstered Glock that was normally covered by his now parted jacket.

"What's your problem?" McCurdy inquired, coming almost nose to nose with the red-eyed young man whose brewery breath instantly answered the question.

"You're my fucking problem," the youth replied, barely aware one of his companions in the back seat was tugging at his collar. "The other guy's got a gun," he whispered hoarsely, but the driver was either too drunk or too occupied with McCurdy to get the message. He commenced a stream of verbal abuse that was noteworthy for its creativity, but annoying to the old cop who instantly reached through the open window and grabbed the surprised offender by the throat.

"Anything else on your mind?" McCurdy inquired, holding the young man in a grip that pinned him to his seat and revealed there was still considerable strength in this geriatric apparition. Price – watching the show through the passenger side window – was hard pressed to conceal his amusement, but managed a serious manner as he retrieved a cell phone from a suit pocket and once again called police headquarters. He had decided the driver was in no condition to drive and that his passengers, although passive enough, were not much of an improvement. Meanwhile, McCurdy had released his hold on the driver's throat as a result of an inspired sense of timing or a considerable stroke of good luck. His victim coughed roughly and spewed a great stream of liquid vomit over the steering wheel and dashboard. A moment earlier and McCurdy's coat sleeve would have been drenched by the foul-smelling torrent.

"Oh, crap," the retired policeman said, wondering how he had blundered into this mess.

"Yes, I know," Price, on the other side of the car, commented impatiently into his cell phone. "I know this is my second call tonight, but there's no goddamn law against it. Get someone over here or we'll release these lunatics and you can take blame for the results." Sobered somewhat by events, the three passengers – one in the front seat near Price and two in the back – had begun to understand that these white-haired men were somehow connected to the police department. The exact nature of the connection would remain a mystery to them, mainly because Price and McCurdy knew they had exceeded their authority and promptly deserted the intersection as soon as two squad cars, red lights flashing, arrived to handle the situation.

"Going to dinner with you is a little like going to war," McCurdy observed to Price as they drove away and he noticed in the rear view mirror that several officers had collected the little band of drunks outside their car. "I doubt you saw this much action when you were on active duty."

"It beats shuffle board," Price replied and let it go at that.

Later that evening, Price sat alone in his darkened living room , sipping a scotch on the rocks and breaking his self-imposed limit of two drinks in a single 24 hour period. "Rules," he thought as he mixed the drink, "are made to be broken." In this case, he broke the rule in response to the memory of Diana Hornbeck, who had shared hundreds, perhaps thousands, of drinks with him at the end of as many days. He had loved the woman for a quarter century and had assumed she knew it when he actually spoke the words as she lay dying in a bed at Ste. Mable the Immaculate hospital. "You are an emotional buffoon," she told him with affection just before she lapsed into a coma and soon afterward went wherever people go when their bodies have given out on them. "Don't leave," was the last thing he said to her, but there really wasn't much she could do about it.

Price had experienced a deep sense of loss when as a teenager his parents had been killed in an automobile accident. The additional loss he felt when the aunt who subsequently brought him up died at the hands of a homeless junkie was mitigated by a quiet rage that compelled him, some thought, to track down the killer and beat him to death with his gloved fists. But Diana's passing had a far more subtle effect on this policeman who had seen death in a great variety of forms. His thoughts of her evoked a wistful sadness that combined with specific recollections of the good times they had enjoyed together. He missed her profoundly but understood that their prolonged relationship had been a fine stroke of luck on his part.

"Here's to you, Honey," he said, raising his glass in a toast to the darkness, and then finished the drink. He put the empty glass on the table next to his chair and settled back comfortably with the intention

7

of shortly going to bed. Instead, he slowly lapsed into a deep sleep in which his thoughts of Diana were eventually transformed into a recurrent dream of Lord Horatio Nelson at Trafalgar. He heard the raging sea battle, smelled the acrid gunpowder and saw the hail of shrapnel and lethal splinters – exploded parts of the ship – that filled the air and ripped through sailcloth and human bodies alike. And he noticed the Admiral's face bore a striking resemblance to a somewhat younger Bill Price.

Chapter Two

Bill Price and Diana Hornbeck never discussed marriage in the entire 25 years of a relationship that was extraordinarily close in a somewhat detached manner. They didn't talk about a formal union because they were each quite content with an arrangement that enabled them to be together or separate, depending on their particular preferences at any given time. Although they usually spent their nights at Diana's condominium, Price maintained an apartment that housed his model ships, books and the miscellaneous stuff he had accumulated over many years. He did keep a small inventory of personal items – shaving gear, underwear, a few shirts and a single navy blue suit – at her place, and she, similarly, had a modest stash of essential things at his apartment. The arrangement suited them to the extent marriage seemed a contrivance that would unnecessarily complicate their relationship, although they understood this reality in an intuitive rather than an actual way. They had come together originally for sex but had soon developed a strong bond based on compatible natures and respect for the other's values and intelligence.

Price fondly called Diana an "unreconstructed smart ass" and she called him a succession of profane names with, he knew, equal fondness. These expressions of attachment were supported by their mutual preference for a couple of vodka martinis before dinner, either at her condominium or at The Bristol, and discussions that ranged from his current investigations or her work to geo-political matters.

She also shared his appreciation for the occasional limerick, but only when it had special qualities. "While Titian was mixing rose matter," he recited to her on the night they met at The Bristol, "he espied his model on the ladder.

    Her position to Titian
     suggested coition
    So he mounted the ladder and had 'er."

Diana remembered the limerick for the rest of her life, but could not recall the way in which Price had worked it into the conversation. "There are some things that don't fit neatly into the average discussion and that's one of them," she once thought. "It's a little like a particular Spanish idiomatic expression, La vida es sueno, which means life is a dream. It has a compelling sound, but it isn't anything you can say to anyone." She had learned the language as a girl in a Central American country, where her diplomat father had been stationed for several years and where, as an early teenager, she had met a young revolutionary in the town square and impulsively run off with him to the jungle. Over several weeks, she managed to get deflowered, which was her intention in the first place, as she and a band of scraggly insurrectionists evaded government troops, venomous snakes, clouds of nasty insects, thick underbrush and torrential rainstorms. With incredible luck and help from indigenous people, Diana eventually made it home safely with the contrived story of her kidnapping and daring escape. Her parents and the authorities bought the big fib, but to her complete distain and everyone else's relief she was soon sent off to a New England boarding school. She later told Price she had been "deported to the tundra." She also related to him an edited version of her "kidnapping," which omitted the part about her young revolutionary lover, but Price put two and two together and surmised the truth. It was a truth he kept to himself because it was history and had no bearing on their life at the time.

A good student who got along with those she liked, Diana eventually went to a state university where she made superior grades as well as a graduate instructor and a full professor. She had a curious mixture of practical and independent notions, which were sometimes at odds and occasionally got her into minor scrapes with school administrators and, later, with several vice presidents at advertising agencies where she worked on the way to her own vice presidency with a firm whose president recognized genuine competence and was willing to abide what one critic described as her "excessive candor." Along with general good looks, which included gray-blue eyes and a slender figure, that quality was the one that caught and held Price's attention over a quarter century.

Despite the long duration and closeness of their relationship, they were essentially private people who kept certain things to themselves. Price had his own secrets, Diana had hers and they both respected the other's right to disclose or withhold anything that had no bearing on their lives together. Price deduced that Diana's teenage romp through the Central American jungle had not been a virginal interlude, a conclusion he drew from inconsistencies in certain elements of the story she told from time to time. He was, after all, a detective. But she had left him completely unaware of the single most important event in her life, and the one he would not discover until she had been dead for almost three years.

Throughout her life, Diana had strong sexual instincts tempered by an inability to suffer those she deemed stupid, humorless or simply uninteresting. This quirk of nature no doubt saved her from a number of bad relationships, but it wasn't flawless in that respect. As a senior at the state university, she seduced a professor in the history department, partly because she was attracted to his lectures on the European Renaissance and Reformation and partly because she hadn't been laid in some time. The man – married with a family and sundry other responsibilities – proved a suitable lover over the short term, but something of a problem in the long run. He was sufficiently potent to leave her pregnant and insufficiently willing to leave his wife, which perfectly suited Diana. She had no interest in marriage, particularly to an ambitious academic who would surely expect her to maintain a household and entertain his colleagues over the long years it would take him to achieve some pedantic goal. "Screw that," she thought as they broke off the relationship and she decided without telling him to have the baby and give it up for adoption.

At the time, Diana's parents had been dead for two years, both killed in a small rebellion in an even smaller African country where he had been dispatched by the State Department. Her father had spent his career in diplomatic backwaters, not for lack of intelligence but more for an excess of candor. It was a trait that had not served him well and one he had passed on to his only child. He had also passed on a modest but sufficient estate that enabled his daughter to live comfortably enough during the pregnancy and to get on with her life once the child, a son, had been born and placed for adoption. She put the event behind her as best she could and never spoke of it, not to Price or anyone else, but thoughts of the child and his subsequent life lingered for the rest of her years. That son and his fate were in her thoughts when she died.

And while Price had not the least suspicion Diana was a mother, he knew there were events in her personal history she had kept to herself. He was aware of certain blank spaces in the biographical information she revealed over many years and in countless cocktail hour conversations, but he had never questioned her about those apparent omissions. He had his own private recollections and was perceptive enough to understand that he didn't need to know everything about the woman. He knew enough, he figured, and let it go at that.

Price eventually learned about Diana's son, but only because the son learned about him at the conclusion of a long search for his biological mother. In his 30s, Andrew Masterson had his adoption revealed to him some years earlier but had been unable for some time to identify his birth mother as the result of sealed and imperfect records that obstructed his efforts. His adoptive parents – good people, prematurely dead from natural but separate causes – had told him about the adoption and the little they knew about his real mother. They had never met Diana and the smattering of information revealed to them was mostly wrong. Masterson, however, finally managed to have the birth records unsealed when new state laws were enacted for that purpose, and the discovery of his birth mother's name set him on a path that soon led to her identification. The man found his mother only to learn she had died as prematurely as his adoptive parents. And in the course of unraveling Diana's history, he discovered she had more or less lived with Bill Price for many years. Given that revelation, it was inevitable he would contact the one person who probably knew his mother better than anyone else.

"Andrew who?" Price inquired of the stranger on the other end of the phone line.

"Masterson," Andrew replied. "I'm Diana Hornbeck's son, and I understand you and she were close for many years." He wondered if he had said too much too soon in the conversation.

"Is this some kind of joke?" Price asked. "If it is, it's not funny." Masterson quickly assured him it was no joke, and went on to generally explain the situation. Price, given his nature and background, was naturally suspicious, but agreed to meet with the stranger for lunch the next day. He had little else to do, and dining with someone other than McCurdy would be a novelty.

They met at The Bristol Bar and Grill where Price was able to identify Masterson from among a small group of patrons who had arrived simultaneously near the traditional lunch hour. The son – just under six feet in height with gray eyes and neatly trimmed brown hair – bore no physical resemblance to Diana that Price could detect, but there was something in his bearing or general manner that seemed remotely familiar. If nothing else, he was reminiscent of his mother and it was a quality the old detective noticed immediately.

"You're Masterson and I'm Price," he said, shaking the man's hand and nodding in the direction of the dining room where he had reserved his customary booth. He didn't reveal that Diana had shared the space with him so often that her ghost, if there was one, would surely be with them that day.

"You come here often?" Masterson inquired.

"You might say that," Price replied before they began a long conversation that eventually established Masterson's credentials as

13

Diana's son. At the outset, the tone was more like a police interrogation than a luncheon discussion, with Price asking the questions. No fool, Masterson understood and respected the older man's careful appraisal of the situation. It was clear to him from the beginning that Price would reveal nothing of substance until he was convinced he was the genuine article.

Finally, Price realized beyond any reasonable doubt that Andrew Masterson was Diana's son, and he provided the younger man with a verbal biography that covered the quarter century he had known the woman. He also commented on certain events before they met, but was careful to explain that Diana was not one to rake up the past.

"I really know very little about her early years, although we had long and detailed conversations for all the time we were together," Price said. "She never mentioned you, although I suspect, knowing her, that you were probably on her mind, at least from time to time."

Price learned from their initial conversation that Masterson's adoptive parents had been decent, middle class citizens who had brought him up in a decent, middle class suburb not far from Chicago, where Diana, coincidentally, had begun her advertising career. Like Price, he had played high school football and gone on to serve a hitch in the Marines. But unlike Price, Masterson earned a degree from a small but respected private college and was eventually recruited by the Federal Bureau of Investigation, where he now worked as a field agent in one of the east coast offices.

"You're a fed?" Price asked rhetorically, aware the tone of his voice disclosed something bordering on contempt for the agency. He had dealt with the bureau on a number of occasions during his long police career and had been at odds with its people more than once. He had also been at odds with his own department more than once, but failed to see the implication.

"It's not as bad as you think," Masterson said, mildly amused by an attitude he had experienced before from local and state policemen who thought their federal counterparts created more problems than they solved. "Some of us have done useful work from time to time." Price had no way of knowing that Masterson had not only done useful

14

but very dangerous work on the agency's front line.

"I'll take your word for it," Price replied without conviction, but in a friendly manner. He liked the man, partly the result of his restrained directness, but mostly because he was more than likely Diana's progeny. For Price, Masterson's presence retrieved in some strange way a vague semblance of Diana's presence, although it was a feeling he would not have put in words. As for Masterson, he liked the grumpy old detective who, he knew, had apparently loved his mother for many years. Price, he also realized, was likely the closest contact he would ever make with the woman who had borne him and he could never know.

They talked well into the afternoon, slowly disclosing to one another the generalities that composed their lives as well as some of the attitudes that revealed their individual personalities. Price noticed that Masterson had Diana's candor, but seemed far more contained than his acid-tongued mother. He was a good listener, and he was particularly intent on gathering information, not only about Diana herself but also anything that related to her family or background. Although he knew little about Diana's immediate family or descent, Price was able to provide him with clues that enabled the agent to eventually identify his grandparents and to uncover a genealogical record that told him more about his ancestors than anyone needed to know. But that would come later.

Price also promised him a few photographs of his mother and other memorabilia, although his collection of these items was sparse. He retained Diana in his recollections rather than in those possessions, which he thought were of scant value when deprived of her presence. The old detective had never attached much value to material things, which he called "stuff," although he understood that money could provide some degree of independence. That realization had been the sole motivating factor in his slow accumulation of wealth over the years, the result of prudent stock and other investments supplemented by an inheritance from the aunt who had taken him in as an early teenager when his parents were killed in the automobile accident.

Price and Masterson told each other a good deal about themselves as the afternoon wore on, but their talk was mainly about ordinary events and interests. The two men were dissimilar in most respects, but both were reluctant by nature to reveal anything of a truly personal nature. Both of them were also perceptive enough to recognize and respect this inbred characteristic in the other.

As a veteran police officer, Price was interested in Masterson's work with the FBI but the younger man said little to satisfy that curiosity. Price, of course, would not press him openly on the subject, but managed to extract bits of information with little tricks he had learned in hundreds of interrogations. Field agents with the bureau, Price knew, were usually assigned to one or another of the organization's investigative priorities, categories that included counter-terrorism, counterintelligence, organized crime, public corruption and violent or white collar crime. Masterson skillfully evaded most of the questions, but Price knew by the end of their meeting that his new friend was deeply involved in a case that sought to bring down a powerful mid-western mobster and his close associates. Masterson was a prudent and clever young man, but he was only a partial match for the older law officer's enormous experience. There was also the further reality that Price intuitively sought to know more about anyone than they knew about him.

Price had long since paid the check – providing the waiter with a generous tip to compensate for their extended use of the booth – when the muffled ring of a cell phone interrupted the concluding stages of what had been a mutually satisfactory meeting. They liked one another.

"Yes," Masterson said, retrieving the phone from his jacket pocket and listening to the caller for a moment before he replied: "I'll call you later." There was a clandestine tone to his voice that told Price his new friend was speaking to someone other than a law enforcement colleague. It was related to either an undercover assignment or some woman, he figured as Masterson put his phone away and explained he had an early evening plane to catch and would call before his next trip to the city, probably in a couple of weeks. For his part, Price offered to mail the pictures and memorabilia they had discussed, but Masterson

16

asked him to hold the materials until their next meeting. "No problem," Price said, thinking the young man probably had no permanent address other than his FBI field office.

They parted company outside The Bristol where Price had recently trounced the two young thugs and where he had come and gone for many years. The restaurant, in fact, had been a more permanent fixture in his life than the succession of two bedroom apartments that had housed his books, ship models and a wardrobe that was modest by almost any standard in the industrialized world. The apartments had varied somewhat, but The Bristol, despite occasional overhauls in the form of paint for the walls or new fabric for the booths, remained essentially the same. The old restaurant, Price thought as he stood briefly on its familiar pavement, is "a rock of stability in a sea of flux." Pleased with the idea, he strolled off to fetch the car he had parked down the block.

Chapter Three

The Bristol Bar and Grill is the oldest continually operated restaurant in town, opened a little before the turn of the 20th century by an aggressive English emigrant named John Swallow and run to this day by his descendents. According to local legend but unsupported by documentary evidence, the original Swallow was a big, colorful character whose business ethics resembled those of the average 16th century pirate. He had served briefly in the British Royal Navy as a very young man and discovered he had no taste for that hard duty at low pay. Some say he deserted ship in a Caribbean port and found his way to the United States aboard a merchant vessel, which he also deserted somewhere on the east coast. Fed up with the sea, he made his way inland to the mid-western city that would provide him with a home and significant wealth over the next half century.

Swallow opened the restaurant for his own amusement after he had accumulated a fortune, apparently from a chain of illegal betting parlors and several well patronized whorehouses. His prosperity had enabled him to develop a taste for fine food, but he had been denied access to the few good eating establishments in town for his generally boorish behavior. He had occasionally gotten into fistfights with other patrons and insisted on pinching the asses of those women, waitresses and customers alike, he found attractive. And there were only a few that didn't fall into that category. He also belched loudly, passed wind at random and bathed infrequently enough to disturb other diners in his vicinity.

He lavished money on the new restaurant – keen to make it the very best of its kind in the region and certainly superior to those places that had declined his business – and named it for the English port city where he was born. Swallow was a knave and a boor, but he wasn't a fool. He spent heavily on the physical structure, inside and out, but he knew the central attraction would be food and that required the presence of a great chef. He found the man in New York and hired him away from a famous restaurant by doubling his salary and providing him regular access to his best whorehouse. That chef would eventually establish The Bristol's reputation for extraordinary food and he would also marry the attractive madam, Pandora Butterworth, who competently ran that illegal business for Swallow. The marriage endured, at least for a while, perhaps because the couple was happy in the relationship or, more likely, because their perceptive boss realized a successful union would ensure that his prize chef remained in town. Toward that end, he gave them a fine house as a wedding present and presided over their marriage like a proud parent.

The plan worked well enough for a dozen years until The Bristol's reputation was secure and the chef discovered his wife had done his entire male kitchen staff at least once. Her promiscuity had given "Pandora's box" an entirely different meaning. Given the chef's temperamental nature and extraordinary skill with knives, the deception proved unwise for the former madam. The couple got into an argument over her infidelities late one night, and he carved her up like a standing rib roast. Luckily for Swallow and the restaurant, however, there was by this time another chef in the kitchen waiting to replace the original one. And the publicity attached to the murder improved rather than hurt the business. Customers who rarely ate out flocked to The Bristol, attracted to its association with a grizzly crime. Those crowds continued until the chef was hung for his skillfully illegal knife work, but not before establishing The Bristol as the most famous restaurant in the city.

By this time, both Swallow and the restaurant had become Institutions, and the owner's crude behavior had been generally chalked up to some kind of individuality that had taken on many of the aspects of virtue. Older and a bit wiser, he still belched and passed wind in public, but with more restraint and less frequency. And it turned out that the inhabitants of the new century were more tolerant of that kind of conduct, at least where institutions were concerned.

The restaurant's reputation was based on the splendid quality of its food, but it also had a bar business that was both complementary and very profitable in its own right. Swallow understood that his bar customers usually became generous restaurant patrons, often in a single evening, and he was not at all pleased with the introduction of Prohibition, which made the sale of alcoholic beverages illegal, after the First World War. Although he could easily have continued operations without the bar, the prospect went against every instinct of his person and he soon established one of the first and finest Speakeasies in the mid-west. He had a false façade built that divided his place between the original restaurant up front and the illegal saloon in back. And he did it with the full knowledge of the police department and city fathers who, in the main, agreed with Swallow's detestation of the new law. Their attitudes reflected those of the general public – excepting a few die-hard Baptists and other psalm-singers – and the newly formatted Bristol flourished into the 1920s.

The city had always had its criminal element, but the bootleggers and gangsters took on an aura of something akin to respectability, at least at the outset of Prohibition before gang warfare began to leave bullet-riddled corpses in public places. Their ability to supply beer, wine and liquor to a thirsty populace gave them a certain standing in the community, and those associated with them, John Swallow included, achieved a degree of celebrity that was surprising in a society with a legal tradition. The patrons of The Bristol, most of them unaware of Swallow's unsavory past, thought of him as a local businessman, and didn't realize he not only sold alcohol but had a hand in its general distribution throughout the city. In fact, he was the biggest operator in the area for several years and achieved that position, rumor had it, through several selective assassinations and a fair amount of intimidation.

21

Shrewd beyond his competitors, the big restaurant owner achieved a near monopoly in a dangerous business without a gang of his own and without personally inflicting anything on anybody. He worked out deals with the principal gangs in the region based on his long associations with the leaders and with his contacts in the mostly legitimate business and law enforcement communities. He was able to get things done and his personal word carried more weight with those he dealt with than the U.S. Constitution.

Swallow was also smart enough to get out of these illegal enterprises when he realized the FBI had substantially increased the number of agents in its local office and brought in a special agent in charge who made the celebrity fed, Elliot Ness, look like a schoolgirl. His name was Trevor Fitzmorris and he set about to dismantle the local gangs one by one and to send their leaders off to federal prisons or to their eternal rewards, either of which made little difference to this genuinely hardheaded law enforcer. He may well have achieved this goal, wholly or partially, on his own, but that proved unnecessary. Swallow saw the handwriting on the wall and cut a secret deal with the special agent that essentially delivered up several of the city's principal gangsters in return for immunity from prosecution. He was also allowed to operate his speakeasy, which he did profitably until Prohibition was repealed in the early 1930s. The wily old crook managed to accomplish this intricate deception without disturbing his relationships with the surviving gang leaders, and lived comfortably into old age until he was carried off by natural causes. The gang-busting Fitzmorris, however, had died years earlier of peritonitis or some similar affliction, which set in when his appendix burst during a rock climbing vacation in Colorado.

A few years after the repeal of Prohibition and when The Bristol's bar had been restored to its original state, John Swallow retired to a large parcel of land outside the city that he called "The Farm." His large house and extensive property had all the characteristics of a farm except for crops and livestock. There was a handsome barn, rolling meadows and expensive fencing that contained the whole complex. What Swallow had mistaken for a farm was actually an estate.

The active management of the restaurant was given over to John's oldest son, Tim, who was eventually joined in the business by his younger brother, Jim, and the two ran The Bristol quite successfully until years later when their sons, Tim, Jr. and Floyd, followed in their fathers' footsteps. For some inexplicable reason, the sons and grandsons of the old crook were all honest businessmen committed to a variety of civic and charitable enterprises that would have embarrassed the restaurant's founder. Had anyone been familiar with the family's history, they would have been hard-pressed not to believe John's descendents were carrying out some kind of penance for their father and grandfather's ruthless conduct. Not so. The old man was probably some kind of social or genetic anomaly and the sons and grandsons were just regular people who ran a good restaurant.

Bill Price discovered The Bristol in his early days as a city detective when he was called on to investigate a murder on the very sidewalk outside the front entrance where, as an old man, he would thump the two young thugs. Given the distance in time between the two events, the irony eluded Price in his old age, but he found his first murder investigation quite interesting. The victim was a middle-aged philanderer whose middle-aged wife had tired of his philandering to the extent she unloaded a pistol into his chest, stomach and the lower region that was her main target. The dead man was a bloody mess and the case was what was once called "open and shut," given the fact the wife was found sitting on a nearby curb with the murder weapon still clutched in her hand.

"That lousy son-of-a-bitch has cheated on me for the last time," she told Price immediately, simultaneously admitting guilt, disclosing motive and resolving the case in near record time. The young detective had only to record certain details related to the crime, which eventually brought him into contact with Timothy Swallow, Sr., who was managing the restaurant that fateful evening. Price conducted his interview with Swallow – who knew the murdered man – in the booth he and Diana would some years later inhabit at frequent intervals for a quarter century, a period in which the space retained its essential form despite several refurbishments. The investigator liked the general

23

atmosphere in the place, particularly the long, polished wood bar in a setting that was somewhere between functional and elegant. "Nice, but not too fancy," Price thought at the time. That impression brought him back to The Bristol a week later for a dinner that particularly pleased his immature palate and led to subsequent visits that would eventually refine considerably his notion of food. It also made him a lifelong patron of what had become not only a local landmark but a restaurant with a national reputation, not only for its food but for its remarkable durability as well.

There had been no doubt the woman on the curb outside The Bristol had with premeditation murdered her husband. The evidence was overwhelming and she readily admitted her guilt and absolute lack of contrition for the lethal act. She was subsequently committed to jail without bond until the trial some months later where she was found, despite her confession, not guilty. A newspaper reporter who covered the proceedings later asked one of the jurors – who obviously sympathized with the defendant – how they could have reached their verdict, given her confession.

"The judge in his instructions to the jury told us we could believe or disbelieve any part of the testimony," the juror revealed. "We decided to disbelieve her when she said she did it."

The food at The Bristol Bar and Grill remained the principal attraction throughout the years as the result of a succession of long-tenured chefs who tinkered very little with the established menu. The restaurant's other employees, too, were notable for their many years of service, particularly the wait staff headed in Price's time by the imperiously friendly Aldo Carnavali. Sometimes referred to as the "world famous Aldo" by patrons and other waiters, the reference was usually meant as a combination of humor and deference to a man whose urbane personality dominated the dining room where he had worked since shortly after his arrival in the United States from Italy. He had begun as a bus boy with scant knowledge of English and developed slowly into the archetypical head waiter, a figure whose projection of sophistication would have made Noel Coward appear the hayseed.

24

The waitress Grace Goodson was another fixture in the dining room at The Bristol, where she and Aldo had been more or less attached for over 20 years. The couple – who lived across a narrow hall from one another in an apartment building - steadfastly kept their relationship private, but it was an illusion impossible to sustain and one that had long since lost its attraction to anyone likely to gossip about it. Aldo had inadvertently disclosed their closeness one evening when he unconsciously patted Grace's shapely little ass when she passed him in full sight of several other employees. Known among them for her unwillingness to tolerate unacceptable behavior from some of the more raucous waiters, they knew immediately there was something between Aldo and Grace. Otherwise, she would have dumped her heavily laden tray, hot soup and all, on him or waited for an opportunity to do suitable damage at a later time. Their life together, in fact, had been one physical contest after another, broken only by passionate reunions that sustained the relationship from one spat to the next. The other members of the wait staff generally knew when they were fighting, not as the result of their apparent attitudes toward one another, which was usually distant at work, but by the small cuts and bruises on Aldo's face or neck. Grace was not above throwing small objects at her long-time lover and her aim had improved over the years. For his part, Aldo accepted his small injuries as the price one pays for a good woman.

Price had been a long-established patron of The Bristol and was well into middle age when he met Diana at the bar where he had settled for the evening and where she had sought refuge from an obnoxious dinner companion. The man had gotten drunk in her presence, made unwelcome overtures and followed her to the bar in a futile effort to get something anyone but a drunken fool would have known was out of the question.

"Leave me the hell alone," she had said to the expensively dressed man who stood, swaying a bit, behind her bar stool.

"You're going to miss a good time," he replied, apparently unaware he had not only missed the boat but not even arrived at the dock.

"And you're going to miss your puny little manhood if you don't go elsewhere," she remarked without looking at him. He had barely time to grasp the rebuke when there was a tap on his shoulder and a crushing sensation in his left foot. Price had come to Diana's assistance and planted his own right foot on one of the drunk's handmade shoes, smashing its upper and pinning him to the spot.

"I'm going to release you in a second and you can either get out of here or I'll break your face," he said with sufficient authority to make a point that even the drunkest drunk could understand. This one stared at him blankly for a moment, got the message and fled as soon as Price set him free.

"I was perfectly able to handle the situation," Diana told Price, somewhat annoyed by his intervention.

"I have no doubt," he said and returned to his seat down the bar, where he remained until somewhat later when the bartender delivered a drink to express her appreciation for his effort. She had given the matter some thought, noticed he had not expected anything for his gesture, and decided to inaugurate a proper meeting. Price subsequently moved down the bar to a seat next to her and commenced a dialog that would continue over a quarter century. They also spent that first night at her apartment, beginning a physical relationship that would last until the onset of an illness that would eventually kill her.

For Price, The Bristol Bar and Grill was as much a part of his life as his old office cubicle at central police headquarters or the familiar city where he had investigated more homicides than he cared to remember. He knew the restaurant employees as well as he knew his police colleagues, especially the senior night bartender, Willy Sutton Sikes, known informally as Sikes, who was in one important respect the exact opposite of the prototypical bartender. Most people in that occupation are alleged listeners, the recipients of almost everything their patrons are unlikely to tell even their best friends. Sikes, however, was a talker and Price, as a result, knew more about this man than almost anyone else. Given Price's reluctance to suffer fools, there was no doubt an explanation for his willingness to indulge this short, overweight, middle-aged dispenser of beverages, but he could never quite figure it out. He sometimes assumed he was more tolerant of bartenders in general, which may have been the case, but he knew it wasn't a proper explanation. He occasionally gleaned a bit of useful information from Sikes, but more often than not he got rumor and an interpretation of local, regional and world events that any bright 10-year-old would have recognized as pure nonsense. But this bartender knew his craft and poured an honest drink, which might, after all, explain Price's willingness to overlook his otherwise flawed personality.

There had been a time in the early history of The Bristol when John Swallow had been closely tied to the local underworld, but later generations of the family had fallen into honest ways. They knew the more prominent criminals, but only as patrons of their restaurant, just as they knew politicians, police officials and many others. Several local mobsters owned bars or restaurants of their own, and only came to The Bristol for a little variety or on special occasions with their friends or families. They were by and large appreciative customers who never attempted to extort the contemporary Swallows until the arrival in the city of an east coast killer who neither knew nor cared about the local conventions.

Frank Baines had been driven from New Jersey by a consortium of mobs who decided his excessively brutal methods brought them unneeded attention from a variety of local, state and federal law enforcement organizations. These were men who had no objection to murder when it advanced their business interests, but understood it was a last resort and something not to be done for frivolous reasons. Baines killed for simple pleasure and without regard for the consequences and would have been put down by his fellow gangsters had he not managed to cut some kind of last minute deal that cost him more money than he had and forced him to leave New Jersey. As a result, he arrived in the city short of cash and considerably pissed off by the recent turn of events.

Baines was just smart enough to avoid the rackets and territories of established local mobsters, but soon discovered by accident that The Bristol was neither owned nor targeted by the underworld. He had dined there in the course of recruiting new henchmen and took a fancy to the place, which he initially thought might be ripe for extortion. The extraction of protection money from honest businessmen had provided him an income stream in the past and might well work in the new environment if he avoided conflict with the resident crooks. Eventually, however, he decided that approach was too slow and devised a plan to take over the restaurant through the simple expedient of death threats to the Swallow families and demonstrations that the wives and children were vulnerable. Baines also made it clear to the juniors, Tim and Floyd Swallow, that he would not only harm their families but bomb the restaurant out of existence if they went anywhere near the police. Their grandfather would have bombed Baines out of existence had he been similarly threatened, but his two descendents were of a more civilized world. Their fear for their families kept them from seeking police protection, and the suddenness of their predicament left them in a quandary until Floyd remembered that Bill Price had some years earlier relieved them of a thug who had tried to force unwanted business on them.

"I'll call Bill," Floyd told his brother as they sat together in the restaurant office.

"I don't know," Tim replied. "What can one old man do against something like this?"

"That old man took care of a couple of punks on our doorstep, and he knows every cop and crook in the central city," Floyd said. His brother looked doubtful, but he found Price's phone number in his big Rolodex and phoned him anyway. Baines had given the brothers 24 hours to respond and some of the time had already elapsed.

Chapter Four

    Frank Baines knew his mother had been a drug-addicted prostitute who abandoned him as an infant, but he never learned her name or the identity of his father. The sparse information about his mother had only been disclosed to him by an exasperated nun at the orphanage where he was placed and only because his consistently bad behavior had driven the poor woman to that harsh extreme when he, as a 10-year-old, had severely beaten a younger boy. He early on developed the habit of extorting anything of value or interest to him from anyone who was weaker, a task made easier by his precocious growth and a natural, bullying nature. Early on, Baines learned to intimidate his victims into silence and to avoid conflicts with anyone large or strong enough to stand against him. This early success based on what seemed to be a natural criminality set him on a path that began with petty adult crime and eventually to anything from grand larceny to murder for hire. Although he was not particularly smart and managed to get himself arrested on a number of occasions, his relative success as a thug and, later, barely competent criminal operator was abetted by his substantial size and strength. He grew into a very large man with a disposition sufficiently mean to make even his closest associates wary of his unpredictable moods. Once in a fit of rage inspired by a trivial but to him offensive remark, he threw a man into a plate glass window and walked away as the large, potentially lethal shards fell from the frame, missing the victim who barely escaped with his life.

Baines ran away from the orphanage and formal education in his early teens and soon found a form of employment with a hoodlum saloon owner who set him to work sweeping floors and delivering various illegal substances and other things around the declining neighborhood in the eastern city where the young man had to that point spent his life. Freed from the schooling he hated and the nuns who had ruler-rapped his knuckles and other parts for continuing misbehavior, he liked the new-found liberty as well as the pocket money he earned for his efforts. His boss was not particularly pleasant or appreciative, but Baines had never expected those qualities in the people he dealt with and he got along passably with the man for several years.

He initially lived in an over-sized closet at the saloon and later when his earnings increased in a small, furnished room at a nearby boarding house. During the period, he learned a good deal about minor criminal activities, some of it from his employer and even more from observation of the small-time gangsters, petty thieves and con artists that hung out at the saloon. He got to know many of these people on a first name basis, particularly after his employer trained and put him to work as a bartender about the time he reached, almost simultaneously, sixteen years and six feet in height. The bartending work was simple enough, mainly because the saloon's patrons drank mostly beer or shots of whisky and sometimes both in the sequence called a Boilermaker.

The young Baines had no aspirations and would have remained at the saloon indefinitely had his boss not bloodied his nose one evening for pilfering small sums of money from the cash register. In his indignation, the man made the mistake of turning his back on Baines, who took the small baseball bat kept behind the bar for defensive purposes and struck his employer across the back of the skull with sufficient force to induce unconsciousness, concussion and a trip to the hospital. Not smart but smart enough to know he would be held to account for his deed, Baines emptied the cash register and fled the place. He also left that particular city and went to another eastern metropolis where he was able to scratch out a living and develop over time somewhat more sophisticated criminal skills. By the time he reached 20, he had allied himself with a minor gang lord who employed him mainly to intimidate small, generally old or frail, businessmen in another run-down neighborhood. He had also learned to use various weapons, mainly firearms but also knives, brass knuckles and a garrote with which he practiced for some time but never to his disappointment found an opportunity to use.

Throughout his teen years, the police in two eastern cities developed long rap sheets on Baines, but these were mostly petty offenses that were generally ignored as the authorities pursued more serious offenders. He had almost come to believe there was little punishment for crime when he was prosecuted in his early 20s for aggravated assault and intent to do great bodily harm, and sent on conviction to the penitentiary. As it turned out, his incarceration proved to be one of the best career moves in his shoddy, young life.

Once inside the great, gray pokey, Baines showed early he was a thug of unusual abilities, although it almost cost him his life. He endured several deep stab wounds in a confrontation with another inmate, who got himself almost beaten to death by the newcomer who seemed not to notice the blood spurting from his body as he smashed his assailant's face and ribs with his large fists and kicked his groin to a pulp with his prison-issue shoes. This performance was noted by Ivor McCusky, one of the major ring leaders in the prison, whose emissary met Baines several weeks later on his release from the infirmary and brought him into the group. McCusky knew a goon when he saw one, and the young prisoner was, once he recovered, employed as an enforcer in a place where enforcement took more than strength. Some of the men Baines was called on to deal with were easy enough, but others were strong veterans of the weight-lifting room who had their own brutal proclivities and often a good deal of confrontational experience. But the event that had sent Baines to the infirmary – combined with his imposing size, natural strength and inordinate tenacity – had also given him a reputation and a psychological advantage that McCusky had recognized and eventually employed to his own advantage. It also provided Baines with a position in the inmate establishment and the opportunity to explore a great criminal network that would serve him well once he completed his sentence.

He emerged from prison early, not as a result of good behavior but because some judge had noted the ancient correctional facility was filled well beyond its capacity. It had been that way for years and would soon refill because the legal remedy that provided Baines with premature release did little to resolve the core problem, which would likely respond only to fewer criminal convictions or more places to put the criminals. That, however, was not a concept that would have crossed his mind as he employed his prison connections to find an association on the outside that was the criminal equivalent of advancement. He was still a goon, but the pay was good and his employer was a major figure in the local mob world.

It was about this time Baines took an interest in expensive clothes, which he noticed often set the crime bosses apart from their underlings. He gradually assembled a considerable wardrobe based originally on the styles he observed among the bosses and later on his own flamboyant preferences. He liked dark shirts, blue or black, which set off his hand-sewn white or silver ties, and tailored suits in a variety of colors and patterns. This sartorial preference did not go unnoticed among his peers, who soon began to call him "Dandy Frank," although not to his face. Aside from his boss, there were few who would chance offending a man whose reputation for tenacious brutality was based on his prison record and soon enhanced by his work outside the walls.

Less than a year after his release from the penitentiary and in a confrontation with a rival gang member, Dandy Frank – who had during his confinement survived multiple stab wounds – was shot three times, once in the right arm, once in the neck – which narrowly missed his carotid artery – and once in the side. Baines managed to strangle his assailant to death even as the shots were discharged and afterward drove himself to a hospital, where he finally collapsed and was treated for his injuries. There were a few who disbelieved the story, but there was no doubt Dandy Frank had been pumped full of holes and that his antagonist had been strangled to death. That was evidence enough for everyone else with any interest in this seemingly impregnable thug and his release from the hospital less than a week after the event only added to his reputation in the local underworld.

Although known to the police and the city's criminal constituency, Baines was not a familiar figure as far as the general public was concerned. His gathering list of felonies, large and small, were not reported by the press and went mainly unnoticed by law enforcement authorities because his victims, when they survived, understood their continued survival depended heavily on their silence. The fear he generated among those who knew something about his deeds was sometimes misinterpreted as respect, and that was the case with Sandra Black.

A young socialite with a taste for high times in low places, Sandra met Dandy Frank in a mob-owned bar patronized by an eclectic group of thieves and slumming gentry who went there for the music – jazz, usually – and an opportunity to observe one another close up. She was impressed with the deference shown him by everyone connected to the place, and was physically attracted to this large, apparently strong man turned out in an expensive suit. She also attached some mystery to his long silences - once they got to know each other – and was simply unaware he had nothing to say. Baines parlayed her complete failure to understand anything about him into a night in a cheap motel. He would have taken her to the best hotel in town, but she insisted on a dump because it added for her an aura of depravity. For his part, Baines was attracted to an attractive woman from what amounted to a different world. The sex with her was similar to his experiences with a limited series of loose women, young and mature, as well as the occasional prostitute, but her manner and speech were entirely different. He failed to notice her rather limited intelligence, mainly because it was compatible with his own and would in any event have made no difference to him.

Under the mutual assumption their physical attraction to one another would last indefinitely, they decided after a week of sweaty rutting to marry, which they accomplished in a mock civil ceremony that made up for in brevity what it lacked in legality. Baines hired an unemployed actor to carry out the charade under the assumption they could always have a real wedding if the arrangement worked out. Sandra had no inkling of the fraud, but probably would have shrugged it off as an amusement had she known the truth. In the beginning, she was perfectly willing to accept Frank's gruff manners and general inattention when they weren't in the throes of sex, but that changed the first night he hit her as the result of a minor annoyance. Her swollen jaw followed in subsequent weeks by sundry bruises and other Frank-inflicted assaults on the body he had earlier prized told the woman there was little future in the relationship, and she fled the apartment they had occupied for only a short time. Baines had lost his ardor for her, but was unwilling to let his fake wife go on terms other than his own. He tracked her to a motel where she had sought refuge, dragged her screaming to his car where he accidentally beat her to death in an effort to quell the noise. A lone fisherman on the river that ran through town spotted the body a week later and alerted the police, who eventually identified the remains and notified her family.

Desmond Black – Sandra's father and a wealthy descendant of one of the city's founders – loved his daughter but had long since been conditioned to her erratic behavior and extended periods away from home. She had once gone to Europe without telling anyone in the family and reappeared two months later as if nothing unusual had happened. He explained to the police that he had not notified them of her disappearance because her absence was more the norm than anything else. The authorities accepted his explanation and commenced an investigation into the murder, which after a while tied Dandy Frank to the dead woman but without sufficient evidence to bring charges against him.

Baines – who was not smart enough to know fear – had no idea an influential city father, Desmond Black, sought his destruction along with a gathering group of local gang leaders who resented his decision to intrude on some of their rackets in an effort to establish his own independent organization. He saw the fear he readily inspired in most of his victims and many of his associates, but he failed to understand that the mob bosses were not so easily intimidated. Those bosses were not likely to let him extract a living at their expense and they were also annoyed by the police pressure that resulted from Black's influence with city authorities. The dead woman's father, who was a close friend of the police commissioner and other senior officials in the local government, had managed to initiate a campaign against specific criminal enterprises and to notify the appropriate criminal bosses that Baines was to blame. The police began a rolling series of raids on whorehouses, gambling operations and low-level drug dealers that had serious cash flow implications for the local mobsters, who were quick to understand the message Black had sent them. They put out a contract on the renegade's life which failed to kill him but did manage to demonstrate something he had not previously understood. The savage attack that riddled his car with bullets, killed two of his companions and from which he barely escaped suggested he was not as invincible as he had previously thought and motivated him to seek some form of compromise with the bosses he had offended. It was that compromise that took most of his money and exiled him from the east coast in a mood that was even nasty by his standards. He was genuinely annoyed, but he had not really learned much from the experience.

Frank Baines had not the slightest notion of Bill Price's existence on that single day when the old detective learned more about him than anyone else knew. Working mostly on the phone and calling in long-standing favors from a variety of police and other sources, Price quickly assembled a good deal of information on the new thug in town. With his wide exposure over the years to many criminal personalities, he understood shortly into his inquiry that Baines was one of the bad ones. The threats he had made against the Swallow families and the deadline he had set were genuine, Price assumed as he soon formed and set in motion a plan to thwart a looming calamity.

Initially, he phoned Tim Swallow and instructed him to gather the various family members together and quickly move them to a safe and convenient location. They settled on the old farm John Swallow had assembled, mainly because it could accommodate the two families and their arrival at the place would attract little outside attention. The

35

farm land itself had been greatly diminished over the years through the development of surrounding properties, but the house had been maintained in its original condition , first by the second generation of brothers and now by the current ones. They had used the farm as a summer retreat for the families and it seemed a reasonable choice as a safe haven from Frank Baines.

Price thought it unlikely Baines knew about the farmhouse, but arranged an elaborate scheme to transport the Swallow wives and children away from town on a circuitous route under cover of darkness and against the possibility their movements were under observation. He also negotiated with the approval of the Swallow brothers the services of six armed guards who were stationed, two at a time, on a 24-hour basis outside the farmhouse. The guards were all recently retired city police officers who worked for a security firm owned by one of Price's old friends from the force. They were instructed to remain out of sight from the road and in regular radio contact with each other and with a duty officer in their home office, who could call on the county sheriff for backup should the need arise.

Once provisions for the families had been made, Price turned his attention to the problem source, Frank Baines. The old detective knew a thug like Baines would not likely respond to threats or reason, which left only direct force as the means to end the dilemma he posed for the Swallows. Although he much preferred conciliation, Price was no stranger to the use of force, which he had employed many times over his long career in an often violent profession. He was not easily drawn to violence as the solution to problems, but he also understood there were occasions when there were no better alternatives. The impending confrontation with the killer, Frank Baines, was one of those occasions.

"Yeah," Baines said into the phone as he reclined on the bed in his room at the Brighton Hotel.

"My name is Price and I represent the Swallow family," he said directly, not only identifying himself but notifying Baines that he knew where he was. Price had discovered his location and knew as well he had not yet been able to assemble henchmen enough to call his handful of goons a gang.

"What are you, a friggin' lawyer?" Baines replied.

"What I am is none of your business, but what I know about you and what you don't know about this city would fill a couple of big books," Price told him in a level tone. "I suggest we talk about it."

"Why not," Baines agreed after a moment's consideration. "Since you know where I live, you can come here."

"I don't think so," Price said and suggested they meet in a small city park not far from the hotel. They were to come alone in two hours and in their individual cars. The meeting would be held on a public bench in full view of the pedestrian traffic that was the norm during daylight hours. Baines gave the proposal some thought. "Okay," he said eventually, "how will I recognize you?"

"I'll find you. I know what you look like and I know what you drive," Price informed him. The information might have aroused suspicion in someone with less brute confidence than Baines, but he operated with the absolute assurance of a man who verged on the stupid and had gotten away with a great deal during his tough life. He had no fear of Price and simply assumed he was nothing more than some business associate of the Swallows. And the Swallow brothers, he was confident, were too concerned about their families to alert the authorities.

"This little talk will be the last thing I have to say," Baines warned as he concluded the phone conversation. "I expect some results from you or Timmy and what's-his-name," he meant the Swallow brothers, "are gonna wish they'd never heard of me."

"I'll see you in the park," Price said.

Chapter Five

George Masterson and his wife, Patricia, had often told friends over the years that their adopted son, Andrew, was too good to be true. They were only partially joking. The child had come to them, newly born and robustly healthy, when they were both in their early 30s and they survived long enough to see him earn a college degree with honors and select a career with the Federal Bureau of Investigation before the adoptive father suffered a premature but fatal heart attack and his wife, only a year later, was struck by a car and followed her husband to wherever.

The Mastersons were moderate to an extreme, which put them in the middle of the road in everything from their political and religious beliefs to their prudent financial dealings and traditional apparel. They were even moderate in their attitudes toward immoderation, which they viewed with reasonable tolerance so long as it wasn't expected of them. They were genuinely good people who treated each other with respect throughout a fairly long marriage, and their temperate behavior had, no doubt, a positive effect on Andrew as he grew up.

There was also the possibility the young man had a genetic predisposition to candor inherited from his birth mother, Diana Hornbeck, and her father, the diplomat whose career path had been stymied by his general lack of diplomacy. Andrew from early childhood on said what he thought, but did it with such grace he was rarely disliked for telling people what they didn't want to hear. And that was the case with adults as well as his childhood friends with rare exception.

One of those exceptions was a neighborhood bully who misinterpreted Andrew's mellow nature, when both were about 10, for weakness. The bully – whose power stemmed from early growth that made him bigger and stronger than most of his peers – sensed Andrew had no fear of him, which was a gnawing aggravation in his bully's craw. As a result, the bigger boy launched a series of verbal assaults on his nemesis, using insults and taunts that he delivered between classes and after school for a matter of weeks and usually in the presence of other students. Andrew ignored him – not out of fear but a distain that was apparent to everyone, including the bully – until a day when the verbal abuse was replaced with a physical form of the same thing. The bigger boy pushed him from behind down a short flight of stairs in the school building and stood above him as he lay momentarily stunned on the landing. His back pack, which he took off as he soon got up, had broken the fall and prevented serious injury.

"I'm sorry," the bully said mockingly before he realized Andrew was coming up the staircase and only moments before his smaller adversary had grabbed his collar and thrown him down the steps to that same landing. As he lay there, stunned and on his back, Andrew descended the stairs, sat on his chest and delivered a single blow to his nose, leaving it bloodied and providing him with a bump on the back of his head when it bounced off the cement floor. The exchange, which took a few minutes, was witnessed by only a handful of others but was soon common gossip throughout the student body. The episode ruined the bully's reputation, made Andrew something of a hero and contributed to his election that year as class president. And while there is no proof, the collective recollection of the event among his fellow students probably followed him through middle and high schools. That remembrance combined with his other good qualities made him quite popular and electable to almost any school office he chose.

Among those other good qualities were his athletic abilities, which were above average but not spectacular. He took what talent he had

40

and got the most out of it through disciplined work and sheer single-mindedness in the achievement of goals he had selected for one reason or another. The effort gained him school letters in football as a running back and captain of the team in his senior year, and in wrestling and track. Although not wealthy, his adoptive parents subsidized his athletic and other extra-curricular activities during his high school years and he worked summer vacations, usually as a life guard at a public swimming pool or when he was old enough as a construction laborer, to accumulate funds for college. The construction jobs were also chosen to build strength and to supplement the weight-lifting program he maintained for the same purpose. In the beginning, Andrew toughened his body for school sports, but later continued a practice he saw as important in a law enforcement career. "I want to be stronger than the felons," he had once confided to a friend.

The young man predictably did well at the small but respected private college he attended, putting his efforts into academic work to the exclusion of athletics on which, he explained to that same friend, he had "overdosed" in high school. Originally, he had thought in terms of a military career, but some branch of law enforcement had become an option as the result of a life-altering event during his junior year at college.

The brutal rape and murder of a young woman friend was Andrew's first realization that no degree of innocence or virtue exempted anyone from the evil that was abroad in the world. He had known Melanie Newcomb since their freshman year, although their close relationship had been platonically based on similar chemistries. They had often attended the same classes, studied and gone together to movies and other forms of student amusement. Their distant closeness, in fact, made Andrew an initial suspect in the case until the investigators learned he had an iron-clad alibi for the period in which the murder was committed. He had been hundreds of miles away on a trip with his parents and within almost constant sight of more witnesses than the police cared to interrogate.

For reasons that were never clear to Andrew, the county sheriff who began the investigation came to the conclusion the murderer was an outsider, a predator who had come to a small college town to vent his vile lasciviousness. The sheriff, who had not previously investigated a homicide, mucked up what evidence there was and ignored the fact the murder scene, which was the victim's dormitory room, showed no signs of forced entry. It seemed probable to the state police who later took over the case and to Andrew that the murderer was either a dorm resident or someone with regular access to the place.

The state police investigation was competent and thorough, but largely unsuccessful until Andrew, several months after the crime was committed, identified for authorities a principal suspect who later confessed to the murder. The man was a drifter who had been employed as a janitor at the dormitory, and Andrew eventually recalled that Melanie had mentioned him on a single occasion. She had described the man as "strange" and said he had engaged her in several conversations that seemed suspiciously contrived. Once this memory came to him, Andrew commenced an investigation of his own and learned the janitor had left his job shortly after the murder. It seemed inconceivable to him the sheriff could have overlooked an event so obvious, but that was the case and he reported the matter to the state police who put out an all-points bulletin and soon captured the man who, it turned out, was wanted in Montana for another rape. The offender was a grungy, deranged person of middle years whose derangement was only apparent on very close examination, a circumstance that explained his ability to gain non-professional employment with the college. Easily captured in a nearby town and only marginally aware of his crime, he was subsequently convicted and given a life prison sentence since the state had long since closed a system of mental hospitals that would have provided a much harder punishment for the insane killer.

This rudimentary investigative experience sparked an interest in law enforcement for Andrew, partly because it achieved some justice for his murdered friend and partly because he found it interesting. His contribution to the case - which was put on record by the chief investigator for the highway patrol – was later a factor along with his academic, athletic and other achievements in his eventual selection by the FBI as a candidate for training. But first he joined the Marines.

Andrew knew the FBI drew candidates for its law enforcement branch from college graduates with at least three years full-time work experience in law, law enforcement or the military, and he could fulfill the requirement through his enlistment and service. He subsequently completed officer candidate school at Quantico, Virginia, where he later attended the FBI Academy.

At the time of his commission as a second lieutenant in the Marine Corps, Andrew had for a time thought in terms of a military career rather than police work. The opportunity for travel and adventure, he assumed, was more likely in the Corps than in an FBI assignment to some domestic field office. But he failed to realize that even the Marine Corps had offices where tedious administrative things were done to maintain and advance the organization. The young man discovered otherwise when he wound up in a succession of desk jobs that had little relation to the intensive combat training he had received at officer candidate school. He had earned his commission at one of those rare times when there was a scarcity of combat situations, a lucky accident that would only occur to him years later and after he had seen his share of violence and death. The circumstance, however, finally convinced him to serve out his hitch and seek a career with the FBI. "Surely, the criminals aren't likely to go away any time soon," he thought in the course of making the decision. The thought wasn't in any respect profound, or even serious, but it was entirely correct.

Not long after his discharge from the Corps, Andrew passed the written, oral, medical and psychological examinations that gained him entry to the FBI academy and its new agents' training unit, where he underwent 17 weeks of hard instruction in a range of subjects from firearms to forensic science. He emerged from the program with high marks earned with his usual native abilities and single-minded application to the task at hand. That performance gained him early assignments to larger field offices where major investigations were conducted into organized crime, bank robbery, kidnapping, drug trafficking and other activities that were both illegal and often anti-social.

By the time his parents had died and he had identified his birth mother, Andrew was a seasoned field agent who had worked a number of important cases from offices on the east coast and in the Midwest. Only weeks before his initial meeting with Price, he had been assigned to an ongoing investigation into a criminal syndicate that was based in an eastern city but had ties with a similar Midwestern organization. He had been selected for this particular case because the illegal activities – which ranged from drugs and prostitution to extortion and murder for hire – were based in the two cities where he had seen service, and were conducted by organizations with which he was marginally familiar. He knew them only because they had tenuous connections to another mob he had infiltrated, and he was selected for the new assignment because an undercover agent on the case had been discovered and executed in a particularly brutal and bloody fashion. His murderers, it turned out, thought he worked for a rival gang and had no notion they had killed a federal agent. Had they known, the result would have been just as terminal, but the manner would have been more discrete. They would have dispatched him with a single bullet to the back of his head rather than hacking his body into several parts to send their rivals a message. They succeeded only in confusing those rivals and substantially increasing the FBI's eagerness to bring them down.

Andrew had for several years worked under cover, passing himself off as a small-time criminal despite an appearance that would have more readily suggested a promising young stock broker. He had managed this unlikely charade because he came to understand the popular notion of a thief is not necessarily accurate and the thieves themselves, observing one another, knew this simple truth. There are both affable and morose killers, not to mention the ones that fall somewhere between those kinds. The same principal applies to all varieties of crooks, which the crooks knew and which generally explained Andrew's ability to penetrate these criminal organizations.

Andrew's manner, too, was unflappable and he made no effort to change his appearance or manner of dress, aware the men he sought

44

to apprehend were not characters out of "Guys and Dolls." Some of them, he discovered, came from middle class backgrounds and few had been driven to crime by poverty, although the real reasons for their anti-social activities would have kept a slew of behaviorists busy for a long time. His interest in their motivations was minimal, limited only to when understanding of that sort provided insight that would give him some kind of edge in a dangerous business or further an investigation.

The specialists in the Bureau who devised Andrew's criminal credentials also fabricated a simple resume for him that would have been difficult for anyone to dispute. This record claimed no jail or prison time which his criminal bosses could easily check, and included his Marine Corps service against the possibility he ran into someone who had known him during that period. But the falsified record, which provided an explanation for his mock descent into crime, gave him a bad conduct discharge for beating hell out of a staff officer and the strong suspicion of other misdeeds. By the time he met Price, Andrew had insinuated himself into the local underworld of the eastern city Dandy Frank Baines had fled to avoid certain assassination. He knew Baines by reputation only and had no inkling of the monumental coincidence that had brought the killer into contact with his new friend.

The qualities in Andrew Masterson that attracted everyone else also recommended him to most of his criminal associates, who generally liked his quiet manner and feigned loyalty as well as his apparent intelligence and, oddly, perhaps, for a crook, his work ethic. He was obviously no goon, and those who employed him found work suitable to his abilities, a circumstance that had so far spared him the need to kill or maim someone as proof of his worth to the organization. There was no shortage of goons in this particular city, but there were few who displayed the cool competence Andrew was able to demonstrate with background assistance from his real employers. The FBI gave him intelligence on rival mobs that enabled his organization to muscle into segments of profitable rackets, and other information, carefully dispersed and given credible sources, that made the agent seem exceptionally useful to his gang. This usefulness didn't go unnoticed by the new underboss of a rival mob, a man with a substantial criminal record who had reclaimed his old position following release from the state penitentiary.

Ivor McCusky – who had recruited Frank Baines in prison and sponsored him on his release – had also put out the contract that nearly killed the renegade thug. Baines had originally been useful to McCusky but not essential. The underboss needed muscle in his businesses, which was readily available, but he also needed smart underlings and they were in short supply. This scarcity drew his attention to Andrew Masterson when his gang was dispersed by the federal prosecution of its leadership. McCusky had no notion, of course, that Andrew had been instrumental in that prosecution, and saw him only as an unemployed crook who was smarter than most of the others in his line of work. Andrew's background – which McCusky investigated through his extensive criminal contacts – seemed inconclusive to the shrewd underboss. There was too little information on which to base a decision about the man, but his local reputation was sufficient to justify a meeting between the two. The call Andrew received during his extended lunch with Price had confirmed that meeting, and the agent had flown east to further, if possible, the new investigation.

"How did you get into this business?" McCusky inquired of Andrew, who he knew as Andy Anderson and who sat across from him in the large booth at Figaro's Trottoria. Two of the underboss' henchmen were stationed at a nearby table, out of earshot but close enough to insulate him from intruders.

"I didn't have much choice," Andrew replied. "My bad conduct discharge from the Marine Corps made it a little hard to find a job."

McCusky peered intently at the young prospect, whose clean-cut appearance and quiet manner seemed at odds with the purpose that had brought them together. "You don't seem like a bad conduct kind of guy," he observed.

"Yeah," Andrew said. "I've been told that." He went on to explain the reason for his fight with a staff officer, other offenses and discharge, a complete fabrication that had been carefully constructed, rehearsed and retold to the point where it had almost taken on the nature of truth. He had put the officer in the hospital, Andrew told McCusky, because the "son of a bitch" was trying to get him brought up on charges for "theft and a few other things."

"Did you do any of those things?" McCusky asked.

"Sure," was Andrew's response, "but that's beside the point."

McCusky smiled, something he rarely did. "No," he said, "that is the point." He went on to explain he didn't want anyone working for him who wasn't, at least, a thief and, preferably, a lot worse. "If you come to work for me," he added, "I'll surely ask you to steal and that would pretty much be the easy part." Andrew nodded agreement but explained he wasn't a killer. "I'm not against it," he said in reference to murder, "but I'm not good at that kind of work." McCusky told him he had other people to handle "that kind of work," which was something they "rarely" did and only when it was absolutely necessary. "It attracts too much heat," he said. Andrew was tempted to ask for a definition of "rarely," but thought better of it. His interviewer sustained a quiet manner throughout their conversation, although the agent detected an inner hardness that was apparent but not easily defined. He also noticed tattoos on both of McCusky's large, rough hands that probably dated to his prison confinement. The artwork was crude, Andrew noticed, and probably done inexpertly by some anonymous inmate.

They talked at some length and neither man made a commitment, but the meeting seemed to go well and it also seemed probable the underboss would bring the FBI agent into his organization, although he had been intentionally vague about the work. Andrew understood, however, that an offer, once it was made, could not be rejected. McCusky, he knew, would not likely take "no" for an answer.

Andrew's patient nature stood him in good stead during the next week he mainly hung around a seedy hotel room waiting for a call, which finally came from one of McCusky's associates. "The boss wants to see you this afternoon," he said, and gave Andrew directions to an address in one of the city's many run-down neighborhoods. Later that day, McCusky brought him into the organization under generous terms and introduced him to a large, quiet man, "Big Al Moroski," who would serve as his boss and "show him around." At the same time, Andrew thought the long wait for McCusky's answer had something to do with local affairs. He didn't know the underboss had been in the Midwest on quite another matter.

Chapter Six

Desmond Black, whose daughter Sandra had been murdered by Frank Baines, was tormented by her loss and the reluctant realization his permissiveness had probably been a contributing factor to her death. His deep love for an only child whose mother had died when she was four made it all but impossible for him to deny her anything that wasn't completely preposterous. She had been pretty her entire life, but even the father recognized that nature had gifted her in that respect to the exclusion of reasonable intelligence. She wasn't a moron and her intellectual deficiencies were never immediately apparent, but she was certainly dumb by any standard of measurement. "Daddy, do you think I'm smart?" she had once asked her father.

"Yes, honey," he lied. "You're the smartest girl I know." She accepted his answer as fact, although she was old enough at the time to know better.

Desmond Black was bred to arrogance in a tradition more reminiscent of the 18th century English aristocracy than the American east coast reality in which he grew up. He was certainly pompous and insular in his relations to common folk, but he was also trustworthy to a fault as a matter of honor and courageous on those rare occasions in his life where courage was at least noteworthy if not absolutely necessary. He had once dived into a flood-swollen river to save a young girl from drowning and at another time had pushed through a crowd of idle onlookers to stop a very large man from publicly beating a stray dog. He had done those things not so much out of sympathy for the victims, but more because it seemed the honorable course of action.

Black concealed his feelings about the death of his daughter, just as he had suppressed a variety of emotions his entire life. He came from an old family whose conservative values mandated a rigid stoicism that had been psychologically encoded on succeeding generations in the male line. Early on, they learned to keep private matters to themselves and to contain any deep emotional impulses they might stumble across. They were taught to seek leadership and power in the community, sponsor charitable enterprises, particularly when there were beneficial tax implications, and to mistrust the unwashed multitudes. Desmond Black accepted all this intuitively and kept his inner rage, directed to the man who had almost certainly murdered his daughter, to himself. He had, in fact, pondered various actions against Dandy Frank Baines – who had been identified as the likely but unproved killer in the police investigation – and knew he would one day use his considerable influence to exact appropriate revenge. It was not justice he sought, but as yet some undefined retribution that would inflict a punishment on the offender so terrible as to render the whole matter settled. Black was no fool and knew, of course, that wasn't possible, which in large measure accounted for the time he had taken to think about the matter. As a result, he had not arrived at any conclusion when he received a phone call from a retired police detective who knew a good deal about the case despite the fact he lived and had worked half way across the continent in a large Midwestern city.

Bill Price had learned a good deal about Frank Baines from an east coast police source, who not only told him about the Sandra Black murder but about her influential father. Price learned that Desmond Black had a formidable reputation and close ties to the top echelons of local business and government in the city his ancestors had settled. "I think this Baines guy will eventually get what he deserves," the source told Price, implying Black was not likely to let his daughter's murderer go unpunished.

50

"That's swell," Price told the man, but explained the urgent nature of his inquiry and as a result was given Black's emergency cell phone number. The fact Price had access to the number told Black the caller had credentials enough to warrant his attention.

"Who are you and what do you want?", the dead woman's father inquired in a voice that showed little curiosity. Price – who had called the man to gather information and, perhaps, provoke action - explained the nature of the threat Baines presented to the Swallow families, and connected the predicament to Sandra's murder.

"The situation is certainly regrettable, but what do you expect me to do about it?" Black asked.

"Nothing for now," Price replied and explained he simply thought Black, given his improbable connection to Frank Baines, might be interested in this turn of events. He assured Black that Baines would not be allowed to harm the two families, but unsaid was the suggestion the eastern power broker might be inclined to initiate some remedial force of his own. Price didn't know the man well enough or have sufficient time to depend on him for a solution to the problem, but correctly surmised that Black, despite his reserve, had a more than casual interest in what he had been told. For that reason, Price divulged detailed information about Baines, including the hotel and room number where he lodged and the time and location of his impending meeting with him in the park. Price had devised his own strategy, not only to protect the Swallows but to end the threat once and for all, but he saw advantages in bringing others into the deadly game. Should the need arise to simply erase the threat with a gunshot or some other instantly lethal means, the development of a list of prime suspects might be a good idea, at least from his point of view.

As Black listened to Price and maintained his natural reserve, he also made notes with the slender gold pen and small pad of paper he habitually carried in the inside breast pocket of his tailored English jacket. He carefully recorded the information in the neat penmanship that was forced on him at the exclusive private boarding school he attended as a lonely but self-contained young boy. The fact he listened to the old detective at some length without interrupting him revealed

51

the interest he tried to conceal, but the extended period of the phone call and the information it provided also gave Black an opportunity to evolve his own plan.

Given his social position and despite his political connections, Black, not surprisingly, had no contacts in the local underworld and probably would have considerable difficulty conducting a simple conversation with one of the mob bosses. They evolved in worlds so different from one another as to preclude any serious communication about anything beyond the weather or directions to some nearby destination. But the patrician knew people who either had direct contact with important underworld figures or the means to reach them through other intermediaries. In particular, he knew a prominent attorney who quietly represented several crime bosses in legitimate business matters without serving their interests in open court where his reputation might suffer for the association. The lawyer, Peter Huggins, was a partner in a prominent firm that had handled Black family matters for many years. He had also handled several personal matters for Desmond Black that required more direct action than the legal system could provide. In turn, Black referred a number of his wealthy friends, some with important corporate attachments, to Huggins as payment for services neither man wanted on the law firm's books. The arrangement had served both men well, providing the client with solutions to several difficult problems and securing the attorney law business that generated prestige as well as substantial fees.

Originally, Black had used Huggins to discourage a blackmailer who threatened to expose one of his late daughter's sordid escapades. The lawyer handled the matter with great discretion as far as his client was concerned, which meant the threat disappeared along with the blackmailer. Actually, the young man who had tried to extort money from Black suffered two broken legs along with sundry bruises and left town as soon as he was sufficiently ambulatory to get away. These details, however, were spared the over-protective father, who in any event was interested only in the result. And that was inevitably the case when he called on Huggins to handle some sensitive matter that defied ordinary solutions.

Pete Huggins was not above employing thugs on those rare occasions he needed them, but he made certain there was great separation from that tawdry business and his mainly wealthy and socially prominent clientele. He also made certain his mob connections were restricted to those few hard men whose legal work he clandestinely handled and that they were always indebted to him rather than the other way around. It was a tricky business, but he was clever enough to carry it off for many years.

One of the lawyer's principal contacts in the underworld was Dominic Chino, who headed one of the more successful criminal enterprises in the city and who sought with little success to pass himself off as a legitimate businessman. He did, in fact, own several legitimate businesses, which didn't really fool anyone who knew anything about local crime, including the police, but which enabled him to justify, particularly to tax authorities, the income that sustained his reasonably affluent lifestyle. Dom Chino and Pete Huggins carefully avoided public contact with one another and used others on those rare occasions one of them sought something from the other. On those exceptionally rare occasions when their business mandated personal contact, they tried, not always with success, to meet under circumstances that would have credited some established international spy organization.

"You're lookin' well," Chino said to Huggins, who approached the park bench where the middle-aged, balding gangster sat carefully manipulating a waffle cone to avoid spilling strawberry ice cream on his dark blue suit. It was a pleasant, sunny afternoon at the municipal zoo, where a handful of mid-week visitors strolled leisurely past them toward the open polar bear exhibit in one direction and the reptile house in the other.

"I doubt it, but thanks," Huggins replied, taking a seat next to Chino and unfolding a copy of the local daily newspaper to give the impression he had sat down only to read. The lawyer, too, wore a dark blue suit, but that was the only similarity between the two men. Huggins was tall with a full head of graying hair and a manner that suggested he had not often sat on public park benches. In the distance, some unspecified animal, probably male, dispatched a plaintiff bellow, an expression, perhaps, of general frustration, antipathy to confinement or, more likely, bestial horniness.

"What's up?" Chino inquired between licks on his melting treat.

"I've got a job that requires your personal attention," Huggins said, his face obscured from general view by the newspaper. He went on to tell Chino that "certain people" want Frank Baines "handled" and he knew "there are others who probably feel the same way." His allusion to "others" was a direct reference to Chino and his associates, who had tried to kill Baines and had finally settled for his exile from the city and a cash payment that had strapped him for money to the extent he sought recovery at the expense of the Swallow brothers. Huggins knew a good deal about local mob affairs, just as Chino knew "certain people" were Desmond Black alone. He knew Baines had murdered Sandra and that Huggins did law business with her father. The connection was not hard to make for a man smart enough to survive in an environment full of savvy operators.

"I heard Baines reached an agreement with some local people that sent him elsewhere," Chino said, fully aware the lawyer understood he was talking about himself.

"I know," Huggins responded, "but there's no law that says the agreement has to last forever." He suspected the only thing that had kept Baines alive this long was the distance between him and his old gang. Huggins sought to eliminate distance as a factor by providing Chino with specific information on Baines' whereabouts and the promise of several hard to acquire city licenses that would lend legitimacy to some of the crook's marginal businesses.

"I'll take it under advisement," Chino said, reflecting his frequent exposure to judicial language as he finished his cone and licked the sticky end of several fingers on his right hand.

"When will I know?" Huggins inquired, folding his paper.

"You'll know," Chino assured him, looking away to continue the allusion they were strangers on a park bench. Luckily for them, the anomaly of two men in dark business suits in the middle of the zoo on

54

a warm afternoon had garnered no attention from the other visitors, who presumably had their own personal concerns.

Dom Chino knew instantly he would accept the Huggins proposal, but was not inclined to show the considerable extent of his interest in "the job." The business licenses were minor inducements but the real attraction, both men knew, was the opportunity to get Frank Baines for his insolent ingratitude. Chino would have done the work for nothing, but Huggins threw in the licenses to make the arrangement a business transaction rather than a favor. These subtle distinctions had kept the lawyer free of entanglements with the underworld that would have made his complicated life even more difficult.

There was one man in Chino's organization who wanted Baines dead more than his boss. Ivor McCusky had brought him into his gang when the two men were in the state penitentiary and later as an underboss in the Chino mob had hired him on his release from prison. He saw the Baines defection as a personal insult, which Baines, had he been smarter and less reckless, would have recognized as a death warrant. Ivor McCusky was no dumbbell, but he was also a thug's thug. He had once in prison cut the tongue from a living snitch. The allegation the man had given information to the warden had not been proved but the suspicion was sufficient for McCusky, who usually dealt with matters straight away.

Chino, of course, was well aware of the festering hatred McCusky felt for Baines and also understood he was perfect in other respects for the assignment. Aside from his hatred for the man, McCusky was the only one in the organization mean and tough enough to handle Baines by himself. He viewed the opportunity to kill Baines – which he could not do without approval from his boss – as a rare opportunity to set matters straight. But when he got that approval later on the day Chino and Huggins met in the park, he kept those feelings to himself. "Anything else?" he asked.

"Have a nice trip," his boss replied, leaning back in an old office chair and using his short legs, planted firmly on the desk, to balance himself. He had laid out the assignment and passed on the information Huggins had given him, particularly the hotel and room number where Baines was lodged. He also told him what little he knew about the threat Baines made to the Swallows, but that was a mere side issue to both Chino and McCusky. Their purpose was to dispatch Dandy Frank Baines and they cared not whether the Swallows lived or died.

Desmond Black had suggested some urgency to the lawyer, Huggins, who passed the message along to Chino and, consequently, McCusky, who was on a westward bound plane before the day had passed. He traveled unarmed – given the airport security measures – with the intention of acquiring an untraceable weapon, ammunition and other articles from a reliable mob connection, who responded to a phone call from Chino and met McCusky when his plane landed at its destination. In less than a day, the event Price had quietly begun in a conversation with Black put a determined killer within a few miles of the man who threatened the Swallows. It was a testament to the power of hatred and to the speed of modern air transport.

McCusky, who had traveled the east coast from New England to Florida, had never before crossed the mountain chains that had once made western travel a considerable chore. He had known people, mostly men he met in prison, from other parts of the country, but geography had not been one of his interests until this trip aroused in him some minor curiosity about the outside world.

"What do you people do for kicks?" he inquired of the stranger who met his flight, a big, quiet man whose few words had not yet disclosed a southern accent transplanted to the Midwest.

"We usually fly east and kill somebody," the man replied, his hands loosely gripped on the steering wheel and his eyes on the road as they drove away from the airport bound for an obscure rental car lot across the metropolitan area. McCusky missed the joke entirely but noticed the accent.

"Where you from?" he asked.

"Mississippi," the driver informed him.

"Ain't that a river?"

"Probably," the man responded, depressing the accelerator to gain speed when they entered the broad belt highway that would take them to McCusky's rental car and the lethal equipment that had been stored in the trunk for him. By this time, he had abandoned the idle conversation that was not only foreign to his nature but, he finally realized, not very productive. They drove in silence, both men intent on his own thoughts and oblivious to the uncountable car lights that rushed toward them on the adjacent highway, until they eventually reached an off-ramp that led to a particularly seedy neighborhood and a darkened building that housed the rental car office. "Some dump," McCusky thought as the driver parked the car, got out and beckoned him to follow on a path into an area confined by a high, chain-link fence where several dozen nondescript sedans were randomly stationed. The man, whose key had unlocked the sturdy gate, apparently knew his way around the premises, which told McCusky the business was mob owned and the rental cars were probably a front for other more profitable activities.

They trekked to the back of the lot where a late model black Buick, recently washed, was parked against the fence. His escort, who gave him a set of keys, suggested he examine the contents of the trunk and check the car for its general suitability, which he carefully did. "When you're done with it," the man said, meaning the car, "leave it at the airport." He gave McCusky specific instructions about a drop-off place within walking distance to the terminal and then inquired: "Anything else?"

"Yeah," McCusky replied, closing the trunk lid. "How do I get to the Brighton Hotel?" He needed directions in this unfamiliar city and was unconcerned that the man might later relate his visit to the murder he had come there to commit. He knew Chino had cleared the matter with this man's boss, and only an idiot or a fool would have mistaken his visit for anything benign.

But he waited, never-the-less, until he arrived at his downtown destination before retrieving the gun, ammunition and a black leather holster from the trunk. Standing alone in the dimly lit hotel garage, he meticulously inspected and then loaded the weapon, careful to ensure he was alone in the vast concrete structure. He then checked its heft and put it, almost ceremonially, into the holster he had attached to his belt. The added weight under his suit coat, while slight, made him feel whole again as he walked briskly to the elevator that would take him into the hotel.

Chapter Seven

"You're a lively old goat," Mimi Swallow said to Jack McCurdy as they embraced in a darkened and remote upstairs bedroom of what the Swallow family called "The Farmhouse," a building that was far too large and elegant for that modest reference.

"I may be old, but I'm not dead," McCurdy relied softly, embracing her firmly enough to announce the erection responsible for her comment. "And you are one in a million," he added, not in the least embarrassed by what he knew was an outright lie. But the middle-aged mother of two was more than attractive enough to justify some distortion of reality, he figured without dwelling on the thought.

"We shouldn't do this," she said, aware she was the one who had led him into the bedroom on what was supposed to have been an inspection of the house for security purposes. Her words derived from some earlier concept of morality or, at least, decent behavior and had nothing to do with her current intention, which was clear to both of them.

"Sure we should," McCurdy responded, kissing her eagerly as they edged closer to the large bed in uncoordinated movements that vaguely resembled a dance step devised by some incompetent choreographer. He knew her protest was a mere formality and their union was as inevitable as his willingness to participate in it. They both knew her sister-in-law and their joint accumulation of children, four in all, were elsewhere in the vast house, but that was an entirely different reality that made no difference to them at the time.

McCurdy had been dispatched to the Swallow estate by Bill Price, who instructed him to check the guards on duty at the place, make certain the premises were generally secure and to reassure the family, principally the two wives, that everything possible had been done to protect their persons and their interests. He had gone there with perfectly good intentions and with no notion of bedding anyone, particularly a much younger woman who, he later thought, could have done a good deal better had she been a bit more patient. McCurdy's opinion of himself was realistic – perhaps the result of his long career in an investigative occupation – and the thought one of the Swallow wives would be interested in him was as foreign as the Gobi desert. Later, he would understand it was only his male presence at a particular moment and not his great charm that had motivated a normally constrained woman to behavior that was completely out of character for her. She had just learned her husband had conducted a long affair with her sister-in-law, Mona Swallow, the woman who had met McCurdy at "The Farmhouse" door on his arrival less than an hour earlier.

McCurdy, of course, had no inkling of that motivation as they abruptly reached and fell onto the bed, where he soon discovered on lifting her skirt that she had either removed or neglected to wear an undergarment. He had no way of knowing she had targeted him for seduction when they met in the large front entry hall, and had excused herself for a few moments afterward to remove and discard that conspicuously absent article of apparel. Eventually, she would reveal these details to McCurdy, whose liberal nature allowed him to appreciate what he considered his great good luck.

Mimi Swallow, more than likely, would have selected a much younger lover had one been available at the time, but McCurdy's presence along with his sturdy manner and affable disposition made him, if nothing else, acceptable. And his later performance – which she thought remarkable for a man his age – made continuation of the relationship, at least for a while, a not unattractive prospect. For his part, McCurdy was an experienced and thoughtful lover, but her evaluation of his capacities probably gave him more credit than he deserved. She had been a virgin when she married Tim Swallow and had never in her life, until that time, been with another man.

"That was wonderful," she told McCurdy as they lay on the bed, both satisfied by the enterprise.

"I'd say so," was his response, aware they had better get on with the house inspection before one of the several employees on the premises or a family member blundered into the room. He helped her up and they chatted casually and hurriedly dressed. She noticed with some surprise that their clothing was not badly wrinkled, a condition that might have aroused Mona Swallow's curiosity had it been otherwise. Not that Mimi cared about Mona's curiosity or anything else about the woman who had, as she uncharacteristically told McCurdy later, "screwed that faithless oaf." The discovery of her husband's infidelity had come as a sudden and complete surprise, revealed by an anonymous phone call shortly before the two families were taken to their country refuge. A man who had muffled his voice provided details of a prolonged affair between Tim and Mona Swallow that was beyond reasonable dispute. He knew things no stranger was likely to know, and in a relatively short discourse convinced her of the long-running deception.

"Who are you?" was the only question she could muster in response to a revelation that was stunning in its own right and came at a time when she and her family were under threat from some criminal force she barely understood.

"That's not important," the informant said, surely aware it was, and hung up.

The two wives and their children had been driven to the country in separate cars from their separate homes, and had only been together for a relatively short period when McCurdy arrived at the house. But Mimi Swallow had thought intensely about the issue on the two hour drive to the so-called farm, and had arrived at several conclusions by the time the families met at their destination. She had managed her anger and her impatient children as she decided divorce was not the immediate answer to her dilemma for a variety of reasons, some emotional and others financial. And she had decided not to confront her unfaithful husband or her treacherous sister-in-law, at least for the immediate future. She concluded that prudence demanded a more leisurely consideration of her prospects, and that reciprocal infidelity would, for the moment, provide a measure of payback to the spouse who, she thought, had not even bothered to screw someone outside the family. "I'll fix both of them," she thought, but had not yet figured out how to do it.

Jack McCurdy, of course, was entirely ignorant of the domestic situation that led to his unexpected union with Mimi Swallow, nor did he wonder to any great extent about those circumstances. He simply zipped up his trousers and continued the home inspection with his newfound lover, although he did arrange a meeting with her for some unspecified future date. McCurdy then carried out a thorough inspection of the premises and simultaneously conducted a random conversation with the woman he had just engaged in a more intimate way. Their conversation was a form of mobile pillow talk that gave the new relationship a degree of validity it would have lost had they simply gone their separate ways immediately after the event. They had, in fact, added to their mutual attraction by the time they returned to confront Mona Swallow and the children with McCurdy's assurance that everything was in order and there was nothing to fear. He was momentarily tempted to ask Mimi Swallow for a second tour of the house, but knew immediately the idea was dangerously stupid. Instead, he excused himself and left to interview the guards posted outside the building. "I'll keep in touch," he announced to the assembled Swallows as he left through the large front door.

"Please do," Mimi replied in a manner that suggested they were likely to see each other again.

Mona detected something in their attitudes toward one another that would have aroused her suspicion had McCurdy been a younger man. There was also the further point she had long regarded her sister-in-law with hidden contempt, an attitude that enabled her to do what she had done without remorse. Mona thought Mimi was too dull and unimaginative to cheat on her husband and, at times, thought that husband, her clandestine lover, was rather dull in his own right. She had taken up with him mostly because he was something of a contrast to his brother, her spouse, and because he was available in an environment where there were few other men. Mona's attraction to the affair had more to do with its titilating nature than to her lover, Tim Swallow. She would have been considerably less interested in the deceit had she known her husband, Floyd, had long been aware of her duplicity.

Floyd learned his wife was involved with his brother early on in the relationship, and considered it one of the great strokes of luck in his otherwise rather luckless life. He subsequently went out of his way on many occasions to make their affair convenient, often leaving town on contrived business trips to provide opportunities for them to meet in a suburban motel. This knowledge, which Floyd kept to himself, enabled him to more easily conduct his own affair with the office manager at The Bristol Bar and Grill, a woman somewhat younger than her boss and lover and a person with a restrained exterior manner that disguised her passionate nature. Over the years, he grew quite fond of the woman, but was unwilling to disturb the convenience of his marriage for child custody reasons, among others.

Floyd Swallow, aware his wife had little attachment to him, had even less attachment to her, which made it possible for him to work with his brother at the restaurant in a way that was superficially normal. They had long since lost those qualities of deep kinship that often account for strong and enduring bonds among brothers, but they were able to function together without rancor and in their joint business interests. And, surprisingly, they were comfortable in the knowledge both of them were honest to the core where the restaurant was concerned. Their personal lives were a monument to deceit, but they were otherwise models of probity.

Jack McCurdy was completely unaware of the Swallow entanglements when he left their family estate and steered his car back to the city. He had interviewed the guards on duty outside the place, and phoned Price to report the situation. His report, of course, failed to include the part where he and Mimi Swallow had sex in that upstairs bedroom. He figured that was none of Price's business, and correctly assumed his friend had little interest in his persistent love life. "You'll screw anything that's remotely female, and I don't want to hear about it," Price had once told him.

McCurdy had know the Swallow brothers for years, but his relationship with them was superficial, restricted to casual and occasional conversation at the restaurant about the weather or the latest news headline. Had he thought about them at all, he would have thought they were just a couple of standard businessmen, good citizens, no doubt, but not interesting enough for extended contemplation . On the other hand, Price knew the Swallows, particularly Floyd, in a far more personal way.

Floyd Swallow had called on Price to extract his family from its current situation because the old detective, more than once, had handled dilemmas for him and done it with effectiveness and discretion. The restaurant owner and his office manager, June Havens, had barely begun their affair some years earlier when her ex-husband threatened to both expose the relationship and to kill them unless he was paid off with an enormous sum of cash. Price stumbled onto the problem quite by accident when he and Swallow became engaged in a casual conversation one night in The Bristol's bar near closing time. Swallow – under considerable psychological pressure and the effect of several drinks to steady his nerves – gradually divulged the problem, which Price had unsuccessfully tried to evade. He didn't care to have other people's troubles dumped in his lap, but this one, once he'd heard it, was another matter. He knew the Havens woman as a gentle, courteous person and immediately recognized her ex-husband for the kind of felonious bully he had so often seen as a policeman. He hated the type, and he told Swallow he would look into the matter.

Bill Price resolved Floyd Swallow's problem within a day, but the exact nature of that resolution remained a mystery to the greatly relieved restaurateur. He only knew that Price called him the following afternoon and explained there was no longer anything to fear from June's former husband, who disappeared from their lives and whose absence made it possible for them to continue an affair that was more constant than most marriages. Swallow never pressed Price on his methods, partly because he knew the effort would be fruitless and partly because he didn't want to know. "Thanks," was all he said to Price at the conclusion of their phone conversation, but his gratitude was apparent in other ways. The hospitality extended to Price at The Bristol was immediate, permanent and comparable to that of an international celebrity. He never had to wait for his favorite booth or service of any kind and his bills would have been absorbed by the house had he not insisted on paying his own way. Tim Swallow never understood the reason for Price's exceptional treatment, but he had his own special relationships with other customers and the two brothers never bothered one another with trivialities.

Jack McCurdy noticed the treatment accorded Price at The Bristol and his comments, early on, often suggested his friend was blackmailing the owners. "I know you've got something on those guys," he once said to Price, "because it sure as hell isn't your personality that rates all this attention."

"You wouldn't recognize personality if it kissed you on the lips," Price replied at the time, but never over the years disclosed to McCurdy the service he had performed for Floyd Swallow. He also never passed judgment on Swallow's affair with his office manager because he thought personal matters of that sort were none of his business. Price considered Swallow a fundamentally decent man, which for the most part he was, and that was good enough for him. His attitude toward Tim Swallow was somewhat different. He didn't exactly dislike him, but sensed something about the man that failed to meet his exacting but rather eccentric standards. This vague suspicion on Price's part was not enough to disrupt reasonably cordial relations between them over the years or to prevent him from assisting the entire Swallow family on those rare occasions they needed his help. Tim Swallow, despite any character or other flaws he might have, was important to Price by virtue of his association with The Bristol Bar and Grill, which in the old detective's life had some of the aspects that churches hold for other more devout souls.

Tim Swallow had been involved with his brother's wife, Mona, for many years and had cheated on her with a series of women, mostly waitresses at the restaurant, for almost as long. The problem with the relationship between Tim and Mona was that it had never been based on any kind of mutual regard, only in the beginning on some frail and transitory physical attraction and nothing else. And when that wore off, there was nothing to sustain the affair other than habit, which for some inexplicable reason kept them together long after either of them had any interest in the other. Had Floyd Swallow not made it so easy for them to make a cuckold of him, they more than likely would have drifted apart years earlier. Although this reality eluded Floyd, he surely, had he known, would have considered it a rewarding payback.

Despite their emotional estrangements from their wives, neither of the Swallow brothers wanted the women harmed as a result of the Frank Baines threat. They didn't love their wives, but Mimi and Mona had given birth to their children and, pending death or divorce, had gained a measure of respect for their painful ordeals. But it was those children that mainly concerned the two brothers and brought them together in an alliance that transcended their indifference to one another. There were two boys and two girls, all pre-teens whose ages were closely bunched and related to the early years of the two marriages when the brothers and their wives were still physically attracted to one another. This batch of brothers, sisters and cousins had been suddenly extracted from their usual lives and brought together for their own protection. Their parents had not explained the situation to them under the assumption a group of nine to 12-year-olds were too young to understand the dangerous implications of their family predicament, which was probably a mistaken notion that accounted for the early rebellion among the children.

"This is crap, pure crap," the oldest boy, Tony, announced to his mother, Mona, within earshot of the others not long after McCurdy's departure. He had been whisked away from his home and school, where he had been scheduled to play in a soccer match. He had never before used that kind of language in his mother's presence but his sudden exile without a reasonable explanation had pushed the boy beyond his normal reserve. Motivated by his protest, the younger children joined him in revolt, each with his or her individual complaint for their detention in what they considered a large, al-be-it comfortable, rural prison.

"Pure crap, pure crap," they chanted in unison, inspired by their somewhat older relative and under the assumption the words had an adult ring. Mimi, perhaps relaxed by her recent experience with McCurdy, was mildly amused by this diversion from an otherwise dreary situation, but Mona was less pleased by the noise and what she considered disrespectful behavior. She was about to dampen the uprising when the insistent ring of a nearby phone had that effect. The children went silent as suddenly as they had done otherwise, intuitively aware the call might have something to do with their circumstances. They stood momentarily transfixed as Mimi, who was nearest the insistent instrument, answered it, and inquired: "Who is this?" She was perfectly aware the caller was her deceitful husband, but the little charade, she felt, was the beginning of her retaliatory campaign. She had no idea, at least for the moment, what that would involve, but she had to begin somewhere. Meanwhile, she listened to the man she now despised and ended their conversation as simply as it had begun. "I understand," she said.

"You understand what?" Mona asked, impatient for any news that might relieve her anxiety.

"We're free to go home and cars will pick us up in the morning," was the reply.

"Yea," the two boys cried once they understood the implications of her response. They also punched the air wildly with their fists and danced around the room like a couple of maniacs as the girls merely smiled to reveal their pleasure.

Chapter Eight

Frank Baines had not expected the bullet that ended his life in the hotel corridor not far from the room he had occupied since his arrival in the city. His killer had apparently waited in an alcove and delivered a single, large caliber slug to the back of his head as he passed in the hallway. The body was discovered sometime later by another guest, a middle-aged salesman who lost his lunch on the corpse, mingling his half-digested burrito with blood that had drained from the gaping wound.

Surprisingly, no one heard the shot that sent Dandy Frank to his eternal destination, which led authorities to initially assume his killer had used a silencer on the pistol that did the deadly work. Not so. The loud report had gone unnoticed mainly because the shooting took place in the afternoon before new arrivals had checked into the hotel and after departing guests had gone. The killer had either timed the event to perfection or been the beneficiary of considerable luck.

There was no way of knowing where Baines was headed when his physical lights were extinguished, but the investigative assumption concluded he was either a very cautious man or had been up to no good. They found two loaded pistols and a large switchblade knife on his remains, a formidable accumulation of weapons that had done nothing to save him from a largely predictable fate. His dead body, face down, lay in the middle of the wide corridor with the palms of his large hands upward and the massive wound plainly visible at the back of his head. It had been this dramatic perspective that turned the salesman's stomach when he unexpectedly stumbled onto the murder scene. The uniformed police officer originally called to the spot and, somewhat later, the detective assigned to the case both had the impression a professional assassination had been carried out, mostly because there was no indication of robbery and the obvious fact the dead man had been ambushed and not confronted. The original assumption Baines had been killed by a professional seemed reasonable enough, but the weapon used in the crime was somewhat at odds with that conclusion. There was no law that said a "hit" had to be done with a specific kind of instrument, but it was more common for people in that line of work to employ small caliber guns that could be more easily concealed, perhaps within the folds of a newspaper, when the work was carried out in congested areas. But this murderer had used a .45 caliber pistol - the handgun equivalent of a canon – perhaps to send some kind of message, but more than likely because the presumptive male was not a professional killer. The investigators assumed the shot had been fired by a man once they knew the weapon was a .45, which usually required masculine strength to handle its weight and recoil.

The late Frank Baines had met with Bill Price earlier on the day he was shot, but that brief encounter in a small city park was more of a confrontation than anything else. The two men – similar in their intransigence and familiarity with death but entirely different in most every other way – had gotten off to a bad start when the surly thug disparaged Price for his age. "What's a tired old man like you doing on a job like this," he had said.

"You can kiss my ass," Price replied and then got directly to the point. "The only thing you're going to get from us is directions out of town." He sat down next to the seated Baines on the green park bench and it was apparent the older man concealed something under a raincoat draped over one arm.

"You plan to shoot me in plain view of everyone in this freakin' park?" Baines inquired. He looked up and down the gravel path where a handful of casual strollers wandered in one direction or another.

"That's a possibility," Price said, and went on to tell him there were no deals to be made. The Swallows, he added, were not about to relinquish their business to him or anyone else, and they were just as unwilling to pay him "a single cent" to leave them alone. "They have more connections in this town than some dumb bastard like you is likely to understand," Price explained, "and the only reason they haven't called in the police is because you're not important enough for anything that drastic."

"I'm going to kill you and then I'm going to kill them," was all Baines said in reply, ending the conversation and standing up a moment ahead of Price.

"Well, then, have a nice day," the old detective called after the angry Baines, who strode off in the direction of the hotel. None of those he passed along the way had reason to notice him or to realize they were the last ones, other than his killer, to see him alive. He had intended to call several local thugs he had induced to join him in a new gang, but had not been able to reach them at that time of the day. He had dallied for a while in the hotel room and had finally in a burst of impatience taken a second pistol from his luggage – which supplemented the one he always carried – and headed off in search of the old man who had recently pissed him off. "I'll fix that worn out . . .," was his last thought as he chugged down the corridor before a large slug made mincemeat of his cerebrum.

The murder of Frank Baines was the lead on all the local radio and television news broadcasts that evening as well as in the morning newspaper the following day. The importance attributed to the event had nothing to do with Baines or the violent nature of his death, which was not all that unusual in a city where common citizens as well as criminals were shot to death on a fairly regular basis. The unusual twist was simply the location, which was the region's best hotel and the place where visiting celebrities from heads of state to rock stars resided when they were in the area. There had been other murders in the Brighton Hotel from time to time over its rather long history – at least by U.S. standards of time measurement – but these events had been few and far between and for the most part a good deal tidier.

71

The most recent homicide, recalled for a newspaper reporter by an 86-year-old shoe polisher in the hotel barber shop, was several decades earlier when the heir to a local fortune strangled his mistress to death in the penthouse suite, creating demand for that accommodation that continued until public memory of the event died away. "He certainly killed the poor woman," the old man recalled, "but it was a much neater job." His reference was to the messy nature of the recent crime scene, which had become general knowledge to those who worked in the hotel. There had also been a number of suicides over the years, mainly distraught individuals of both sexes who flung themselves from windows on the upper floors, but these deaths weren't accorded the stature of murders by hotel employees or the general public for reasons known mostly to people on the fringes of academic life who ponder those things.

Price had early knowledge of the murder – just as he had early knowledge of other police activities – and phoned The Bristol to alert Floyd Swallow to the good news. But he was away from the restaurant at the time and his brother, Tim, took the call.

"Frank Baines is dead, shot to death this afternoon at the Brighton Hotel," Price told him and added it was now safe to bring the two families to their respective homes. He also requested that Tim pass the information along to Floyd, which was inevitable in any event, and that the details would no doubt be on the evening news. Immediately after the call, Tim phoned his wife at "The Farm." Price also called Jack McCurdy who, on learning Baines had been killed, suspected his friend might have done the job. "Did you kill that rotten bastard?" he inquired, inserting the expletive to indicate his approval had that been the case.

"As a matter of fact, I didn't," Price replied. "I'm too old for that kind of thing and there was really no need. There were too many others, I suspect, who were willing to take on the responsibility."

McCurdy heard the response but had no idea whether Price was telling the truth. The two men had been close friends for more than 40 years, but Price – who on several occasions was thought by McCurdy and others to have taken justice into his own sturdy hands – had never confided either that kind of information or anything about his deep personal life to anyone other than the late Diana Hornbeck. And there was a lot he had not told her.

McCurdy knew that his friend, many years earlier, had almost certainly beaten to death a homeless junkie who had murdered Price's aging aunt, the woman who had taken him in as a teenager after his parents had died in an automobile accident. The case in which the old woman had been brutally assaulted and raped in the course of a home robbery was investigated by two detectives sympathetic to their colleague and suspect. They concluded there was insufficient evidence to bring charges against Price or anyone else and the matter was dropped within a few weeks. But the swift and absolute nature of the retribution that descended on the aunt's killer gave Price a reputation throughout the metropolitan police force and in the criminal community that served for the rest of his career as both an advantage and a handicap. To his advantage, Price gained enormous respect – sometimes based on fear – that often furthered his investigations, but the suspicion of his rogue behavior was known in the higher echelons of the police department and surely impeded any advancement beyond his rank as a first class detective.

For his part, Price cared not a whit for advancement, aware high departmental rank was usually supported by political skills he neither had nor wanted. And since prudent investments over a long period supplemented by an inheritance from the murdered aunt had made him financially independent, he remained content with a salary that changed little from year to year. "It isn't money that cranks his engine," McCurdy had once told someone in a discussion about Price.

Diana Hornbeck – without relatives other than the son she had never known – left an estate of several hundred thousand dollars to Price, which he kept separate from his own resources because he neither needed the money nor knew what to do with it. He occasionally pondered its disposition without result until the reality of a legitimate heir to Diana's estate appeared in the form of Andrew Masterson. After their meeting, Price began to think about settling this bounty on the young FBI agent, but had deferred any final decision until he knew more about him. Their long initial meeting at The Bristol had gone well, but Price wanted more information than a first impression, no matter how positive, could provide. He knew first impressions were often accurate, but not always.

Coincidentally, Price had thought about the disposition of Diana's money, which derived from his thoughts about her as he relaxed with an iced vodka in his quiet apartment. He slumped comfortably in his favorite chair, vaguely aware of the failing light outside his front windows when the coincidence – a phone call from Andy Masterson – revealed itself.

"What's up?" Price, who recognized the voice, inquired.

"I know you've been retired for some time, but I have the impression you know what's going on in your city," the younger man said. "Have there been any murders in town in the past day or two, particularly anything that appears gang related?"

"Funny you should ask?" Price responded. He then told him about Frank Baines and the dead man's attempt to extort ownership of the restaurant from the Swallow brothers. He didn't reveal his involvement in the situation and passed the information along as though he had collected it at random from news sources and conversations with old friends on the police force. Masterson revealed he was investigating a man in his jurisdiction that had been dispatched to Price's home town, perhaps to carry out a contract murder. He didn't identify Ivor McCusky or tell the old cop he was working undercover for the very felon who might have murdered Frank Baines. Masterson had learned McCusky's destination by sheer accident, piecing together bits of information from overheard phone conversations and other random sources. He discovered that his boss in the gang had gotten a last minute assignment from the big boss, Dominic Chino, which was a clear indication that something lethal was a real possibility. McCusky – who had gained his position in the mob as an enforcer – was not likely to be sent on a mission that required anything other than brute force. And when Price identified the murder victim, Masterson was convinced McCusky had carried out the assassination either on orders from Chino or to settle his own grievance. The dispute between Baines and his old

74

underworld associate was common knowledge in the Chino mob and even Masterson, who was new to the organization, had heard the story several times. But he kept this information to himself, aware Price would understand the need for complete confidentiality in an ongoing investigation.

"I don't think it was a professional hit," Price told Masterson, unaware the agent had arrived at the opposite conclusion. "Everything from the choice of weapon to the place where the murder was done tells me the killer doesn't do this for a living. The job got done, but it was plain, dumb luck there were no witnesses."

"What kind of weapon?" Masterson asked, but didn't change his opinion about the killer's identity when Price said the work had been accomplished with a .45. McCusky, he knew, was more of a goon, although a rather shrewd one, than a contract killer, and would have used the powerful handgun not only to make a statement but to utterly destroy the man who turned on him. As far as the murder scene was concerned, Masterson assumed McCusky simply picked a time and place when no one else was around, dispatched Baines with a single shot and fled the place, probably down a nearby stairwell to an outside door he had identified earlier.

"You plan any trips here any time soon ?" Price asked near the end of their conversation. He sought an opportunity to further evaluate the younger man before making any final decision about Diana's estate.

"I don't have any definite plans at this point," Masterson replied, "but there's a lot more I'd like to know about my mother." He told Price he would give him advance notice should circumstances or spare time provide a chance to continue the discussion they began at The Bristol. And he thanked him for the information he had supplied on the Baines murder, which he linked to Ivor McCusky. Masterson had no intention of gathering evidence in that case to prosecute McCusky and sought only to learn as much as possible about the tangled affairs of the Chino mob. He and the other agents assigned to the case wanted to bring down an entire criminal operation and were just marginally interested in a single murder, particularly the assassination of an exiled felon who deserved his fate more than most.

75

Price had no idea Masterson was working undercover in an organization that had once included Frank Baines and whose members made an earlier attempt on the thug's life. But it was readily apparent to him that Masterson was working a case that was somehow connected to the Baines murder. The matter was really none of his business, he realized, but the old cop could not put aside the curiosity that was developed over a long career in law enforcement. He did not intend to conduct an actual investigation, but he also knew it was something he was not likely to forget. "What's the lad up to?" Price thought, aware he now wanted to know more about Masterson's work as well as his suitability as heir to his mother's assets.

Masterson's conviction that McCusky had murdered Baines was short-lived. The next day, he and Big Al Moroski – who had been given the task of showing him around the organization – were seated at a table in Figaro's Trottoria near the booth where their immediate boss, McCusky, and the ultimate boss, Chino, were having lunch. Their conversation was muted, but clearly audible to both Masterson and Moroski, who were there to protect the privacy and persons of their mob superiors.

"Somebody got to the son-of-a-bitch before me," McCusky told Chino in a tone that seethed with angry disappointment. "I cased the hotel and decided it was too crowded to do the job inside," he continued, unaware the fork he held in one hand was gripped so tightly his knuckles had gone white. "Some lucky moron shot him in the hotel in the middle of the afternoon and nobody saw a damn thing."

"I wouldn't worry about it," Chino, who had tied a napkin around his neck, consoled him as he precisely carved the steak he had ordered for lunch. "The end result is the same."

Masterson, who listened intently to the conversation but looked away to disguise his curiosity, wondered who, if not McCusky, had shot Baines. The murder, he thought, may have nothing to do with his investigation but it was a mystery that left him with an unsettled feeling. He had not yet learned there were situations in life without explanations. Big Al, meanwhile, gave no hint he had heard anything as he ate with apparent relish from a large plate filled beyond its usual capacity with an undistinguished, marinara-laced pasta. The only mystery that concerned him, although not at that particular moment, was the nature of his next meal.

Chapter Nine

"I don't mean a woman did it," Price explained, somewhat impatiently, to McCurdy as they sat next to each other at The Bristol bar. "I'm just saying a woman can't be excluded."

"You're nuts," McCurdy replied. "Have you ever heard of a woman who killed anybody with a .45?"

"You've been away too long," Price said, meaning his friend had been retired from police work to the point he had lost touch with recent developments, particularly in handgun technology. There was also the allusion women now did things that had previously been the sole province of men.

"And you haven't?" McCurdy posed the question, but knew he was treading on thin ice. His friend, he also knew, had closely monitored the changes in almost everything related to police work over the many years of their retirements. Although he was not likely to admit it, he thought Price could conduct a competent investigation into anything that might confront a modern police department.

"Not me," Price responded and then told him about the development of .45 caliber automatic pistols with manageable grips and other features that made the gun easier to handle for shooters with smaller hands and less arm strength. McCurdy still thought in terms of the stout weapon that was the standard-issue side arm for the U.S. armed forces from 1911 until the mid-1980s. The gun had been widely used in the two world wars and in the Korean and Vietnam conflicts.

Price knew quite a bit about the .45 but kept the knowledge to himself under the assumption McCurdy either knew the same thing or didn't have any particular interest in the subject. Price knew the weapon was a semi-automatic handgun developed for U.S. military units engaged against Moro guerillas during the Philippine insurrection that followed the Spanish-American war at the end of the 19th century. An earlier .38 caliber revolver had proved unsuitable at stopping the tough Moro tribesmen, who were thought to combine high morale, drugs and effective bamboo armor in deadly charges on American troops. The .45, it turned out, delivered sufficient wallop to stop a Moro or Frank Baines, whose corpse remained unclaimed and was eventually buried at public expense in a remote field set aside for that purpose.

"What woman would want to kill Baines?" McCurdy inquired. "He hadn't been in town long enough to get into that kind of trouble."

"I can think of two with motive, although no opportunity," Price replied, alluding to the Swallow wives, Mimi and Mona, who with their children had been threatened by the late gangster. He knew the women were nowhere near the Brighton Hotel when Baines was shot and that McCurdy had met them somewhat later at their rural refuge. He didn't know the extent to which McCurdy had met Mimi Swallow, and it was something his horny friend was not likely to disclose. "I'm sure those women didn't do it, but there's a lot we don't know about this Baines character," Price added. He went on to explain that the murder weapon and the murder scene, which seemed entirely too random to him, made it unlikely the killing had been carried out by a professional. "I can smell this one and it tells me the shooter was an amateur."

"You're the boss," McCurdy said as he motioned to the bartender, Willy Sutton Sikes, for another drink. He also noticed a woman, moderately attractive by any standard, seated several stools away, and in another timeless barroom gesture signaled Sikes to send her a drink, too. The act was one of spontaneous generosity motivated by a pretty face and without expectation of anything other than a grateful

80

nod from the recipient. But McCurdy, as usual, had not calculated the various possibilities. In this case, he did not anticipate the woman's burly companion, who he had not seen earlier and who was relieving himself in the men's room when McCurdy, assuming she was alone, bought her drink. His first indication of the real circumstance came in the form of a rough tap on his shoulder from the man, who on his return from the lavatory interpreted the drink as an attempt to steal his girl friend.

"Who in hell are you?" the man inquired, obviously annoyed and a little drunk.

"What?" McCurdy replied, turning from his drink and only vaguely aware of a situation Price recognized immediately. "It was only a friendly gesture, nothing more," he told the man, who responded: "Butt out, you old buzzard." By this time, McCurdy had swiveled his stool around to confront his antagonist. "You'd better piss off, son, before I ruin your night out," he said.

The remark triggered an immediate response that might have cost McCurdy a broken nose had Price not seen the man's clenched fist and beaten him to the punch. He delivered a left hook from short distance that landed squarely on the side of the stranger's face and dropped him to the floor, where he sat for a moment, stunned by the blow.

"Listen to me before you get up," Price advised, hooking his thumbs in the waistband of his pants, which parted his jacket to reveal, as he had on other similar occasions, the holstered gun on his belt. He had renewed the habit of carrying the weapon during the Frank Baines episode. "We're not looking for trouble and we'll forget the whole thing, if you will."

"Forget the whole thing, my ass," McCurdy inserted before Price stared him into silence. The man, whose attention had been drawn to the gun, rose unsteadily and wordlessly backed away from the two old men. Shortly afterward, he paid his bar bill and left the place with his woman companion. The bartender had witnessed the entire event, which had developed and been resolved with such speed he had no chance to alter its course. Uncharacteristically bereft of words, he shook his head and gave them a round on the house, partly because he felt a twinge of guilt for delivering a drink to the woman without alerting McCurdy to the situation.

"I can remember when you didn't need to rely on a sucker punch and that show 'em the gun trick." McCurdy observed.

"At my age," Price replied, "I need all the help I can get, particularly when I'm with you." He didn't reveal that his left hand, which had delivered the punch, was quite sore. "Goddamn arthritis," he thought.

Bill Price hated physical training of any sort for the boring, repetitive activity it was, but had regularly exercised most of his life, first as a high school athlete and later as a police officer aware that some of the crooks were strong. He knew prison weight lifting provisions allowed inmates to vent energies that might otherwise cause trouble within the institutions, but he also understood that those in law enforcement often had to deal later with a raft of muscle-bound thugs. Price sought to even the contest and did it with a combination of efforts that had long ago developed into habits he continued into his retirement years. He lifted weights, punched a heavy bag and jogged the streets near his apartment, all to appease the endorphins he had conditioned to that expectation and some vague thought it was useful. He also continued to fire his pistol on a suburban range under an assumption – one he had long understood – that there would always be someone stronger than himself.

Despite discipline born of both determination and habit, Price knew his condition, both physical and otherwise, was on a descending slope and that his efforts could only slow and not stop the rate of descent. Even so, he found his capacities, both physical and otherwise, were often better than those of much younger men and women who failed to notice there was not yet dribble on his chin. "Snot-nosed incompetents," he sometimes thought, particularly when younger people with jobs assumed he had nothing to do in retirement and kept him needlessly waiting for one reason or another. "My time," he had explained on more than one occasion, "is just as valuable as yours unless you're working on either a plan for world peace or a cure for cancer." They usually weren't.

Jack McCurdy was no dummy, but subtleties, particularly as they related to people, usually eluded him, and that was the case in his relationship with Price. He knew the man better than anyone alive, but there were many things about him he didn't know. "Price doesn't believe in an eye for an eye," he once observed, "he believes in two eyes for an eye." That was true enough, but over-simplified a complex personality who could administer lethal, although illegal, justice on the one hand and enforce the letter of the law on the other. And, uniquely, Price understood the contradictions in his behavior and lost no sleep over the paradox.

As an early teenager when his parents were killed in an automobile accident, Bill Price was old enough to have extended memories of his mother and father. He had loved them both in his own detached manner, but particularly the mother who had influenced his childhood in ways that were still apparent in the old man. She had instructed him not to fight other children when he first went off to kindergarten and only changed her mind when she discovered an older boy beating on him in their front yard. He took the blows, not wanting to disobey his mother, until she gave him permission. "Fight back, Billy," she said, and her small son beat hell out of the bigger bully.

Price's mother never again restrained her son's natural inclination to defend himself, although, recognizing his natural ability in that respect, encouraged him to also defend, when possible, others as well. Those others, she told him at selected and appropriate intervals, were the innocent weak or afflicted who were unable to defend themselves in a world with too many bullies and scoundrels. And while Price never consciously processed his mother's instructions, her little homilies – given credence by his absolute devotion to her – penetrated to the very core of his nature and influenced everything from his choice of a career to the way he conducted his entire life.

His father, Joe, left the moral instruction to his wife and gained his son's respect and affection through a combination of essential decency and the practice of taking him to ballgames and a variety of movies that would have tested the patience of most other adults. His death along with his wife would have left a gaping hole in the son's universe had not his sister-in-law, Bill's aunt, taken the boy in and assumed the role of both parents to the extent she provided a moral compass for him and a companion at baseball games and the movies as well.

Price's aunt, Mary Elizabeth Speck but known to him as Aunt Moon for some reason he had either forgotten or never known, would have gone to the ballgames even if a nephew had not been thrust upon her. She was what some call a "fan," one of those demented people who follow specific teams in good times and bad and are prone to do foolish things in the process. Aunt Moon, who taught general science in one of the city's high schools and coached the girls basketball team because there were no women baseball coaches in the system at the time, was no exception.

"Kill the blind blackguard," she had once screamed at an empire, but "Kick their backsides" was a more regular cry from this slender, almost delicate, woman, whose behavior outside the ballpark was restrained and dignified to the extent a stranger might have thought the two different modes were evidence of some deep psychological problem. Not the young Bill Price, however, who early on was amused by her rampant enthusiasm and the purple baseball hat she wore, sometimes sideways, at all the home games for the Martins, their local minor league team. Although her manner away from the ballpark was more sedate, she was far less pacific than her sister, Bill's mother. She had a confrontational streak that compelled her to meet opponents of any sort head on, and she encouraged this attitude in her young charge. "Just make sure you're right before you stick your neck out," she advised him on an occasion when she had almost been fired for an intemperate remark made to her school's principal. She called the man a "blind oaf" for suspending one of her favorite students for theft, an accusation she originally thought "absurd" but which later proved embarrassingly true. "So, shoot me," she said to her boss, who, aware her judgment was otherwise quite good and her work at the school beyond reproach, accepted what he liberally interpreted as an apology.

Price's aunt assumed he would one day attend the state university, an assumption that seemed more certain when his high school academic record, while not spectacular, proved good enough to gain him entry and his record as a lineman on the football team guaranteed an athletic scholarship. But the young man – despite an inherent interest in books and a genuinely curious nature – had tired of academic confinement and wanted to see something of the wider world. He decided a hitch in the United State Marine Corps would provide that opportunity and enlisted for four years not long after his high school graduation. "It's your life," was Aunt Moon's only comment, which was her way of telling him it was his decision, not hers. "Just make sure you don't get yourself killed in some God-forsaken backwater," she added, aware there was no war on at the time but with little confidence that state of affairs would continue for very long.

Price soon discovered that military service – while it involved travel – was just another form of confinement, given the rigid system of rules needed to effectively run large organizations. Despite that epiphany, he liked the Marine Corps for reasons he never bothered to define. He even liked Parris Island, South Carolina, where he took his "boot" or basic training with a miscellaneous group of young men in his general age group who had failed to consider the timing of their enlistments. They arrived in the sweltering heat of mid-summer to learn that incessant close-order drills, marches and constant harassment from various sources are more bearable in temperate weather.

One of those sources was a gunnery sergeant who gave them their first inspection when they had only been on the island a week. A formidable veteran in dungarees with military creases, he stood before this group of awkward beginners who barely knew how to shoulder their M-1 rifles. "I hate civilians," he told them loudly, his face an inscrutable mask. "My entire miserable family is a bunch of no good civilians," the sergeant continued. "I hate my entire miserable family, especially my mother."

Aware his immediate fortunes and possibly his life were in the hands of the sergeants and corporals who ran this isolated place, Price restrained the smile that would have had serious consequences. But he, unlike most of the others, knew from that moment on his trainers were a group of serious actors whose performances were meant to intimidate them into submission before the real business of military training could begin. The purpose – according to Corporal Clark, their drill instructor – was to snap them "out of their civilian shit." Price understood what was going on, which gave the experience an element of interest for him that most of the others saw only as grueling drudgery that could not end soon enough.

"This crap doesn't seem to bother you," one of his newly minted buddies observed one day as they sat on the hard-packed ground, bone tired, on a short break from one of their interminable marches.

"I like to sweat," he replied. The physical ordeal was not unlike his high school football training, particularly in late summer practices that most of the others had not experienced. In some respects, he thought at the time, the military stuff was easier. The hard days in the blistering sun and sand pits where they often did close order drill wore him out, but he didn't have to wear football pads or endure the painful leg cramps that awakened him in the middle of the nights until he got into shape for the actual games. And Corporal Clark, who was a wiry combat veteran, reminded him of his old coach.

Price didn't mind the physical aspect of his Marine Corps training, but was really attracted to the variety of firearms that were an essential part of military service. There were no guns in Aunt Moon's household and he had never before fired a weapon of any kind until he discovered on the Parris Island rifle range his aptitude for lethal weaponry. He easily qualified as an expert marksman, which was the result of his sharp eyesight, steady hand and some intuitive quality that defied definition. He was as good, he discovered, with the heavy Browning automatic rifle and the lighter carbine as he was with his standard- issue M-1, and even better with the .45 caliber pistol that later became his particular favorite.

Price never intended to make the Marine Corps his career, but the four years he divided between state-side and duty on a distant but peaceful Pacific island pointed him toward law enforcement. The opportunity to thwart the bad guys – an impulse his mother had sponsored and his aunt endorsed – combined with the chance to carry a gun provided the only motivation he needed to seek and gain entry to the police academy in his home town only months after his military discharge with the rank of buck sergeant.

Price's early years as a uniformed police officer were distinguished by several acts that displayed sufficient courage and competence to win him medals of commendation and an early assignment to the plainclothes detective squad, where he eventually rose to the senior ranks but accumulated a reputation for maverick behavior that impeded his further advancement. He slowly came to believe the municipal system was too inefficient to meet the mounting law enforcement problems in the crumbling central city where he mainly worked and occasionally Price, over time, elected to administer his own brand of justice. These indiscretions were selective and always carefully executed to the extent there was never enough evidence for his superiors to confront, reprimand or punish his suspected behavior. As a consequence, he gradually came to represent something of a problem to those above him, just as his reputation as one of the most effective officers in the city developed in the lower ranks of the police department.

"Anything else?" Willy Sikes inquired of Price and McCurdy, aware their glasses were empty and had been for some time. It was only mid-evening but they were the only ones left in the bar.

"Not for me," Price replied, which was an indication he was ready to pay the bill and go home. But McCurdy had a conversational issue to resolve.

"Do you still have that old .45?" he asked when Sikes had gone down the bar to fetch their tab. Price shook his head in mock disbelief, aware his friend considered him a suspect in the Baines murder. "I didn't kill that miserable felon," he said.

"Answer the question," McCurdy insisted.

"I haven't had that gun for years, as if it was any of your goddamn business," Price explained with a hint of impatience that was more the product of his readiness to leave than the question itself. He went on to explain that the gun he carried, a Glock model 38, was smaller, lighter, easier to conceal and still fired a .45 cartridge. "So," he continued, "you should have asked me if I killed the bastard with the piece still strapped to my belt, and the answer is the same."

"I just thought I'd ask," McCurdy said as he waited for Price to pay the bill.

Chapter Ten

Floyd Sparrow leveled his old Cessna 172 out at 5,000 feet and throttled back to a steady cruising speed diminished somewhat by a moderate headwind. "No matter," he thought, since there wasn't any particular rush other than his desire to see June Havens away from The Bristol Bar and Grill. The weather was good – barely a cloud in the morning sky – and neatly arranged section lines on the ground below him were an assurance his navigation instruments were reliable. He had cleared the strip at Lakeview Airport, where he had hangared his plane for years, and felt the sense of release he invariably realized at the controls of the little red and white aircraft that had carried him to some of the most interesting events in what had otherwise been a rather pedestrian life.

The Baines murder was now several weeks behind him, and his family life had settled into a routine that made it possible for him to get away from the restaurant for a while, particularly since his brother, Tim, was there to represent their interests. The two men had often spelled one another over the years to achieve short interludes, if not actual vacations, and the arrangement had served its purpose. The Bristol Bar and Grill was as intrinsic to their lives as their blood chemistries, but the heavy demands of a complicated and successful business made these breaks increasingly essential for both of them.

The Sparrow brothers were polar opposites in almost every respect other than gender and commitment to the family restaurant. Floyd, tall and spare, contrasted with Tim who was somewhat under medium height and, while not fat, was a few pounds beyond his ideal weight. Their personalities and temperaments, too, were equally divergent. Although both dealt effectively with customers on that superficial level possible with people who were not often together, Floyd was easily the more respected of the two by their employees and those who saw them on a more regular basis. Floyd's manner was direct, his word was more binding than a legal document and he had an intrinsic sense of fairness that governed everything he did. On the other hand, Tim, while honest as far as the letter of the law was concerned, acted mainly in his own interests, often to the exclusion of those who worked at the restaurant and learned over time to distrust the promises he made to dispense with various problems. And, of course, to the exclusion of his brother, whose wife he had clandestinely bedded over a long period of time.

Had Floyd loved his wife, Mona, he surely would have confronted his deceitful brother, severed their business relationship – which would have ruined the restaurant they both prized – and gone off on his own. But he was easily the smarter of the two and realized at the outset that Tim's transgression with Mona was one of those unexpected gifts that are sometimes delivered by sheer chance. Floyd excused his brother's perfidy to protect the restaurant – where their work was complementary – and to avoid the divorce court and what would have been an inevitable custody battle for the children he loved almost as much as he loved his office manager, June Havens. Mostly, Floyd allowed Tim to screw his wife because the diversion made it easier for him to conduct his own affair. Floyd was usually direct, but he was also capable of duplicity when it served a higher purpose.

Only a little after June Havens and his two children, Floyd loved the four-passenger Cessna that had flown him all over the United States and to Canada and Mexico. On this day, his destination was a small airport within a relatively short driving distance of Chicago, where he would meet June at the Drake Hotel. She drove separately to preserve the privacy that would not have been possible had she left with him from the small airport where his plane was kept and where he and his family were well known. Floyd and June had spent many long

90

weekends together in Chicago, which was close enough to their home city to afford a relatively easy commute and large enough to provide the privacy they sought. That privacy, however, wasn't absolute, mainly because Floyd knew hundreds, perhaps thousands, of his restaurant patrons as well as others, and some of them also traveled to Chicago where even long odds would sometimes bring them together in public places.

"Son of a gun, Floyd, is that you?" one of them inquired once, as they accidentally met one afternoon on north Michigan Avenue, not far from the hotel.

"Probably," Floyd replied. "Have you met my wife?" The answer, luckily, was negative because his companion was June Havens. The device of passing his lover off as his wife worked so well he employed it on several other occasions with equal effectiveness. He assumed anyone who discovered the deception was not likely to report it to anyone else, particularly his wife, and if they did he could counter with an accusation about her own duplicity.

Despite the headwinds, Floyd still managed to make the trip in well under three hours, which was his long-established limit for the full duration or a leg of any flight. That limit had been established by his bladder and a reluctance to simultaneously fly the plane and pee into some small plastic vessel. He had long since learned to relieve himself and to drink no more than a single cup of coffee before he took off, enough to remain alert but not enough to create any anxiety when his attention needed to focus on landing the reliable old Cessna. As a result of this prudence, Floyd brought the plane smoothly onto the single paved landing strip at the outlying airport with thoughts of June Havens on his mind rather than the urgent need to find a lavatory. He knew she had left a number of hours ahead of him and had probably checked into the hotel by the time he tied the plane down and retrieved a rental car.

Floyd and June saw more of each other during a usual week than the average married couple. They worked together for years at the restaurant, where they maintained a business-like relationship devoid of the occasional intimacies that could have occurred between them.

They continued the charade because June insisted on it and because their busy schedules often kept them apart within the confines of a single, al-be-it large, building. But even more important was the knowledge they shared that proximity, if not handled carefully, could destroy a union they both felt was worth preservation. This close separation made their occasional trips together more singular, and their intimacies all the more sustainable because it wasn't something available to them day to day.

"It's me," he said, unlocking the hotel room door to discover her in bed with a book, her familiar nakedness concealed with a crisp, white sheet. He carried a small, black nylon bag, which he sat on a nearby bench provided for that purpose.

"I hope so," she replied, putting the book aside along with reading glasses she had recently acquired. "How was the flight?"

"Smooth as glass," Floyd lied because he didn't think a little choppiness was worth the conversation. Instead, he looked around the room until he discovered the inevitable bottle of scotch and an ice bucket she had put on the desk. "Care for a drink?" he inquired as a formality to the preordained and positive response.

"Yes sir," June said, watching as he simultaneously unbuttoned his shirt and put ice into two glasses. He had also removed his wrinkled khaki trousers by the time he added the whisky. And he was completely devoid of clothes – which now hung over the desk chair – by the time he joined her in bed and delivered the drink. He had disposed of his shoes and socks, she noticed, just inside the door.

"You mix a speedy drink," she observed as he placed an arm around her bare shoulder and kissed her, tenderly, on the cheek.

"I do, indeed," he said, aware her leg was against his as they clinked glasses in an unspoken toast to their impending time together. It was a ritual that inaugurated those times and usually preceded several days of repeated sex separated by restaurant meals, occasional walks along the Lake Michigan shore and only enough sleep to sustain the other activities. Floyd had learned that several days of repeated sex - much like his three hour flight rule – was the limit of his endurance. And June, too, found that three days of

92

multiple unions were more than sufficient for her needs as long as the intervals between their meetings were not too long.

"I made reservations tonight at Tony DeAngelo's," he announced at length, resting the glass on his bare, hairless chest, where it left a damp ring. "Is that okay with you?"

"Sure," she said, "as long as no one gets murdered while we're there." The restaurant, rumor had it, was mob connected, but the food was good and the place was lively with a variety of types, most of them respectable but a few with vague auras of criminality. Tony himself, who was a suspected front man for local gangsters, had known Floyd for years and had been to the Bristol Bar and Grill, where the two had developed a cordial if not close relationship based mainly on their similar business interests. DeAngelo, who also knew June from The Bristol, treated her with a certain variety of quiet respect based on what he regarded as her lady-like qualities and professionalism at the restaurant. The pros he knew were generally of another type.

"Sweet Jesus," she cried when after appropriate foreplay he eased himself onto her and was surprised by a reaction he knew was too soon for orgasmic attribution. He had forgotten the cold water his glass had deposited on his chest and that had been transferred to hers when their bodies met.

"Sorry," he said when she explained the situation, and immediately before they came together in an even more intimate connection where recollection of that damp transfer was replaced by yet another mingling of moisture.

Later at the restaurant, Floyd and June were part way through their first drink when they were joined by DeAngelo, who had arranged their seating at one of the best tables in the house. The location afforded a degree of privacy in a busy room as well as an unobstructed view of the entire place, including the long, crowded bar that ran almost the full distance of one side.

"Good to see you folks," he greeted them. The word "folks" was entirely alien to DeAngelo's usual vocabulary, but he was a man who thought anyone from outside Chicago and, perhaps, New York lived next to a corn field.

"Same here," Floyd responded with sincerity because he felt good enough to feel good about seeing almost anyone. The feeling stemmed from recent sexual gratification followed by a sound nap and a hot shower. June, too, felt rested and relaxed for much the same reasons and was content to savor her drink as the two men began a sustained conversation about their businesses. The subject loaned itself to considerable variety, ranging as it did from the rising cost of meat to recent wine acquisitions and the ditsy behavior of certain customers. This talk continued until June excused herself and went off to the restroom, wending her way through a maze of tables that had filled with diners in the time since she and Floyd arrived at the restaurant.

"Did everything work out?" DeAngelo asked when she was out of earshot.

"Just fine," Floyd replied. "I owe you for this one."

"Anything for a friend," DeAngelo said with the false implication there was no debt involved in the favor he had done for someone who was nothing more than an acquaintance. He would one day expect repayment of some kind and Floyd knew this reality. But it was a deferred reality and he was presently satisfied with the progress of his brief holiday. "Anything off the menu that's particularly good?" he inquired of his host as June returned and quietly took her seat.

"Everything's particularly good, on or off the menu," DeAngelo informed him, "but I like the Osso Bucco. My doctor won't let me eat Osso Bucco, but I like it, anyway." The reference was to an arterial condition that was incompatible with fatty meats, which he had enjoyed until his physician put him on a rigid diet he often ignored. "I probably ought to eat all that stuff just to make sure I die a natural death," he joked, alluding to those mob connections he knew were common knowledge among those who knew about such things.

DeAngelo remained at the table long enough to leisurely drink a glass of Chianti and pay florid compliments to June before he excused himself to attend his restaurant business. "Thanks, again," Floyd said as he left.

"Thanks for what?" June inquired when DeAngelo was gone.

94

"The table and our dinners, which I assume are on the house," he responded. The assumption about the dinners was correct but the gratitude he expressed to their host was an entirely different matter he was not inclined to explain. Instead, he turned the conversation to pleasantly trivial matters and she responded in the same general way as they had another drink and then dinner that did not include Osso Bucco. They enjoyed each other's company and the evening went well until June broke the heel of a shoe on the curb as they entered a cab for the return trip to the hotel, where they had left their cars in the parking garage. She also painfully sprained her ankle, but refused to let Floyd carry her through the lobby. Rather, she clung to his shoulder and hobbled the distance from their taxi to the elevator and, when they had reached the appropriate floor, down the hall to their room where she collapsed on the bed. As she lay there, relieved to be off the offending ankle, he drew hot water in the bathtub for the purpose of soaking her injured part. Once that had been done, he returned to the bedroom and sat next to her.

"I think I can live without sex for one night," he told her, assuming the injury had foreclosed that option and letting her know he understood the circumstance. June looked at him as if she were peering over the frames of her reading glasses. "I didn't come here not to do it," she said.

Their trip was barely compromised by the ankle sprain, which turned out a mild one. They walked less than usual, but that loss was easily replaced with activities within the hotel room. Since the purpose of the trip was coupling complemented by moderate alcohol and decent food consumption, they had no difficulty achieving those objectives within The Drake while her ankle repaired itself enough for the drive home.

As they lingered over drinks on the final night of their holiday, seated in matching chairs and considering their food order from room service, Floyd confessed he had told his sister-in-law, Mimi, about her husband's infidelity.

"You did what?" she asked, fully aware of the implications but unable to understand the reason for something that seemed counter-productive from their point of view.

95

"I just got tired of his constant efforts to screw anything within arm's length," Floyd explained and went on to provide details about his brother's latest attempt to seduce still another new waitress at the restaurant. June, of course, worked there and was perfectly aware of Tim Swallow's lecherous tendencies but said nothing as Floyd told her about the phone call to Mimi in which he disclosed his brother's infidelity. He also told her that he had made the call in a disguised voice, a trick that apparently worked but gave June the impression Mimi must have given him the benefit of the doubt. Floyd, she knew, was no actor. "What about Mona?" she asked, wondering how this turn of events would affect his wife.

"I didn't think about Mona," Floyd admitted. "I just did it."

June also wondered what effect, if any, this development would have on her long-term relationship with this man, who was the only lover she had known other than an abusive husband. Floyd, in fact, had rescued her from that painful union. As her boss, he saw bruises she attempted to hide with make-up, uncovered the truth and arranged not only a sanctuary for her but the legal representation needed to achieve a divorce. He also confronted the husband, who disappeared from June's life for reasons that were not entirely clear but which promoted feelings in her that eventually brought them together.

"I'm going to divorce Mona," Floyd said at last. "I can prove she's been sacked in with my ass-hole brother since year one, and that should give me access to the kids." He thought for a moment and continued: "They can live with her as long as I can see them regularly, and we can live together, if that's okay with you?"

She smiled uncertainly, barely aware of the broad changes in their lives that were implied by the relatively few words he had spoken. "Are you sure?" was all she said as a succession of thoughts began to assemble and which might have given her pause had not the jangle of his cell phone interrupted their conversation. It sounded a silly little tune until he retrieved the instrument from the desk where he had left it.

"Floyd here," he said and listened intently for a few moments, his face visibly gathering gravity. "Where, when?" were his only other words before he ended the conversation and turned to June.

"What is it?" she asked.

"My brother's dead," he replied. "Shot outside The Bristol earlier this evening."

Chapter Eleven

Tim Swallow's body was found on a loading platform outside the back entrance to The Bristol Bar and Grill some time after three large caliber bullets to the chest had been delivered from close range. The second and third shots, a coroner later determined, were entirely redundant, considering the first one was more than sufficient to do the lethal work.

He had been dead for a while when one of the kitchen staff – sneaking a short break for a cigarette – found the corpse stretched out flat on his back, eyes still open in a surprised gaze that told something of the story. Swallow had been ambushed on his way to the E-Class Mercedes parked nearby in an area reserved for the two restaurant owners and a few of their more privileged employees. The killer had apparently selected the site for several convenient reasons. There was little traffic in the area at that time of the day, early evening, and there were a number of nearby places of concealment. There was also the obvious fact that Swallow, sooner or later, would retrieve his car. On the day he was shot, however, he left the restaurant far earlier than usual and at a time when business traffic was building and his attendance on the floor was most important. Something or someone might have lured him out of the building while there was still daylight enough for accurate identification, investigators later surmised.

Bill Price and Jack McCurdy, who were dining that evening at The Bristol, were alerted to the murder by one of the restaurant employees who, like all the others, still thought of the two old men as cops. They were the cops they knew as opposed to the ones Price called to the scene once he and McCurdy had chased off the morbidly curious who had gathered about their dead employer, possibly, as Price knew, trampling valuable evidence. Price, too, called Floyd Swallow, unaware he was out of town, with news of his brother's murder. He had simply used the cell phone number Floyd had given him when Frank Baines threatened the Swallow family.

Bill Price was no forensics expert but he had seen enough gunshot victims in his time to realize that Tim Swallow's killer had probably done the work with large caliber ammunition. The dead man in his last act alive had removed his suit coat as he headed for the black Mercedes, and the massive amount of blood on the front of his white shirt gave general witness to the extent of his wounds. Price had ample time to scrutinize the crime scene before police arrived and also noticed there were no shell casings in the immediate area, which suggested the shooter had removed those bits of evidence. "If this wasn't the work of a professional, it was done by a very tidy amateur," he observed to McCurdy, who was mildly annoyed by a murder that had interrupted his dinner.

"I don't know about that," he replied, "but it seems to me this city has gotten a bit deadlier than in our day." Actually, the incidents of homicides in the metropolitan area had come down in recent years, but the assassination of Frank Baines, followed so quickly by this murder, made it seem otherwise. In retirement, McCurdy had put the often bloody business of homicide detective behind him and now the occasional exposure to something that was once commonplace seemed exceptional.

Although he wasn't inclined to express an opinion openly, given the lack of evidence, Price wondered if the murders of Frank Baines and Tim Swallow were related in some way. That conclusion seemed entirely too pat, but it was one that couldn't be ignored, considering the closeness in time of the two events and the use of a large caliber gun in both cases. He was curious to know if Tim Swallow had been done in with a .45 which, if true, wouldn't really prove anything unless

100

the two crimes had been committed with the same weapon.

Price kept those suspicions to himself when the lead detective assigned to the case arrived with several uniformed officers less than an hour after discovery of Tim Swallow's body. Gunther Hagle was a seasoned veteran on the detective squad who knew Price by reputation, but had only been a rookie patrolman when the older man retired. They had not met before but Hagle soon realized that Price, despite his age, had retained the investigative instincts that had made him a minor legend in the city police department. Price's general analysis of the murder scene was complete and his knowledge of the restaurant and its personnel, something he knew from long years of patronage, was incredibly thorough.

"You're a walking encyclopedia on this place," Hagle said appreciatively, aware Price had made his job somewhat easier. He had been given information on everything from the restaurant's ownership to the recent trouble with the late Frank Baines, and had made occasional notes on a small pad of paper he had fished from the inside pocket of his inexpensive navy blue suit coat. "These guys still dress like me," Price thought as he waited a moment for the detective to complete one of his notes. Given the quickness of change in most other respects, he was mildly reassured by something that had remained the same.

"Where's the brother?" Hagle inquired at last, referring to the absent Floyd Swallow.

"I don't know," Price replied truthfully, but without mentioning that he had alerted Floyd to the killing. "I assume he'll either phone in or be here before long because he seldom spends much time away from the business." By this time, the surviving brother had checked out of The Drake and was on his way to the airport for the flight home. June would remain at the hotel overnight and drive back the next day.

A large, bluff man with graying brown hair that displayed the first signs of male pattern baldness, Gunther Hagle sought answers in the smallest details of an investigation. That trait sometimes seemed at odds with his open personality, but it had made him a very effective investigator. Within a few days, he had isolated a number of suspects, among them several members of the dead man's family.

Floyd Swallow had been the first on Hagle's list of possible killers, mainly because he stood to take over the business once Tim's estate had gotten its due and also because the investigation soon revealed the relationship between the deceased and his sister-in-law, Floyd's wife. Floyd, however, was able to establish he was out of town at the time of the murder, which meant he didn't personally fire the fatal shot. But in establishing his Chicago alibi, Floyd also revealed his long-standing affair with June Havens. That attachment suggested to Hagle that this particular suspect had not been motivated to murder by infidelity on his wife's part. It seemed apparent that neither of the marital partners, Floyd or Mona, cared enough about each other to commit a random thought, let alone a serious felony.

The two wives, Mimi and Mona Swallow, also came under scrutiny as one thing led to another in the course of the investigation. Mimi, Hagle speculated, could have discovered her husband's infidelity with Mona, which was an ancient motive for murder that eventually seemed unlikely. Mimi, it turned out, was out of town with her children at the time of the killing, and there was nothing in her background to suggest she had ties to anyone capable of murder. Mona, too, was busy elsewhere when her long-time lover took three robust slugs to the chest, but at least one of her acquaintances, Hagle later discovered, had a criminal record. And the relationship between Mona and Tim Swallow, he learned, had soured, a time-tested motive for any number of illegalities.

Hagle eventually discovered the affair Tim and Mona conducted over many years had fizzled out some time earlier and that both had moved on, Tim to a series of women employed at the restaurant and Mona to a cement contractor who had served prison time for an assault that had almost killed the battered victim. The contractor was Marvin Sylvester, a slick but hard-nosed character who wore expensive suits made possible by his success in a tough business. "What a bloody mess," Hagle thought as he untangled the various relationships, including the affair with June Havens that Floyd Swallow divulged when he established his Chicago alibi. Floyd, however, would have kept June out of it had he not decided to make their circumstance a matter of general knowledge.

In the course of the investigation, Hagle came to trust Price's information about the case, which was the result of his long patronage of The Bristol Bar and Grill and his close association with the restaurant's owners and employees. He also learned that Price may have retired, but his mind still worked like the detective he had been for many years. It was soon clear to Hagle that Price was a good judge of character, and that his judgment made clear distinctions between the Swallow brothers. "Floyd is a genuinely good guy," the old cop told the younger one, "and Tim, if you'll pardon my negative opinion about the dead, was a rat." And while Hagle made his evaluations based on more than a single source, his final conclusions about the Swallow brothers was strongly influenced by information he drew from Bill Price.

Gradually, the lead detective's attention was drawn to Marvin Sylvester, mostly because he had shown violent tendencies in the past but also because he earned his prosperous living in a business that had been notoriously infiltrated by known mobsters. Sylvester's success in a business environment dominated by crooks, Hagle reasoned, suggested he was probably one of them. He also knew from earlier investigations that certain elements among the local cement contractors were capable of murder on those rare occasions when lesser forms of coercion failed to work. In all fairness, however, Hagle had to admit that Sylvester's name had never been associated with any crime other than a single assault, and that had occurred when he was a very young man. He had either gone straight or gotten smarter, Hagle concluded until something more conclusive turned up.

Marvin Sylvester was roughly handsome in a way that either strongly attracted or repelled women, depending on their particular preference. Mona was one of those women who fell in the former category, and became instantly involved with him after a chance meeting outside The Bristol one afternoon. Both had eaten lunch earlier and were leaving the restaurant to fetch their individual cars when they accidentally brushed against one another. This mild collision provided an opportunity for conversation, which soon developed into one of those inexplicable electrical events that often attracts two people. Mona's affair with Tim Swallow, never intense, had long since lost whatever charm it had, and her marriage to Floyd had not been viable for years. She had been unconsciously ready for Sylvester or someone like him for some time, and he, recently divorced by a third wife, was always available to any woman he considered remotely attractive. Mona attracted him with an aura of suburban respectability that covered, but not very well, inwardly slutty proclivities. She was also well-dressed, which was a matter of some importance to a man who valued outward appearance.

Hagle wasn't privy to the details of their initial meeting and the psychology of their attraction would not have interested him, but he eventually learned they came together twice a week at a respectable but locally remote motel, which Sylvester had used for earlier affairs that had contributed to his multiple divorces. Mona had no trouble making excuses for her time away from family and other matters, mostly because her relationship with her husband and his brother had gotten to the point where none of them cared one way or the other. Given this situation, which Hagle eventually came to understand, there seemed no reason for Mona or a surrogate in the form of Marvin Sylvester to kill Tim Swallow. Her husband, Floyd, would have been a more understandable target since his death would have released her from a meaningless marriage and provided a substantial legacy. But the detective couldn't rid himself of the notion that Sylvester or one of his associates had carried out the murder.

Hagle had assembled some of the leads in the case from interviews with various employees at The Bristol who, not surprisingly, knew a great deal about the various relationships and affairs that occupied the Swallow brothers and their wives. Much of it was rumor or speculation, of course, but he was able through meticulous follow-up work to document many of the realities and to discard the other stuff. He learned from two waitresses at the restaurant of their quickie interludes with Tim Swallow in his office, where a couch under close examination showed the remnants of semen stains accumulated over many years. The two waitresses, Hagle concluded, were only the tip of the iceberg.

Hagle, quite by accident, met Price at The Bristol – which had been closed until Tim Swallow's burial - as he returned for further interviews and to gather other evidence. Price was there for meals, either lunch or dinner, on an almost daily basis. At first, they spoke briefly in the lobby or some other common area, but eventually scheduled occasional lunches together to discuss progress on the case. As he came to know Price, Hagle disclosed more details about the investigation and about the Swallow brother's tangled affairs, much of which Price had known for some time.

"Tim Swallow's office was more a bedroom than a place of business," Hagle told Price one day as they sat in his favorite booth and awaited the bill for lunch.

"That's been common knowledge among the employees here for years," Price responded. "They called his office 'Tim's Motel.'"

"Was all that screwing consensual?" Hagle inquired, meaning consensual on the part of the women.

"I suppose," Price said, "although I'm sure Tim used his leverage as boss to get what he wanted." He thought for a moment and added his own question. "Do you think any of these girls have husbands or boyfriends who were irritated enough to whack our late friend?"

"The thought crossed my mind, but I've only identified two of the ladies and I know there are more," Hagle replied.

Price assured him there were many more and suggested he talk to June Havens who could surely identify most, if not all, of the waitresses who had cycled onto the couch in Tim Swallow's office at one time or another. "June is a discrete woman," he said in her defense, "but she'll give up the information to point you away from Floyd."

Price was right about June, although she assembled the list of present and former employees with some reluctance, feeling, as she did, the matter was none of her business. She had never liked Tim and kept his affairs as far removed from her own as possible within the confines of the restaurant. But she was observant by nature and there were some things she absorbed simply because there was no way to avoid the information.

"I assume you'll keep this confidential," June said to Hagle when she gave him the list, written in her own neat hand with addresses and phone numbers, many outdated. She also told him about several incidents over the years in which men confronted Tim Swallow for his loose handling of certain women on the list. To June's knowledge, these confrontations had led all those with disgruntled husbands or boyfriends to quit their jobs, but she could recall no violence attached to any of the episodes.

"Lucky man," Hagle observed, forgetting for the moment that Tim Swallow's luck had run out on the loading platform behind The Bristol Bar and Grill. He thanked her for the list with the assurance its source would remain anonymous, and mentally noted there were more than a dozen names, most of them former employees. He realized it would be all but impossible to locate some of the women – given the length of time since they left their jobs at the restaurant – and it would be even more difficult to identify and locate former husbands, old boyfriends and other incidental men in their lives. Several of the women, however, were still employed in their original jobs, which made Hagle wonder how they made the transition from Tim Swallow's couch to a normal work situation. Price supplied him some time later with a probable explanation. "The tips are good," he said.

The murder of Tim Swallow occupied Bill Price's thoughts intermittently, mainly because he had the notion there was some connection between that crime and the assassination of Frank Baines. His occasional conversations with Hagle also kept the matter alive for him along with his natural inability to forget an unresolved mystery. He thought about the matter on and off, particularly in the evenings when he worked on his latest model of Admiral Nelson's flagship, Victory. Price knew Hagle was assembling a sizeable list of suspects and a small mountain of evidence, which was, he thought, a sign of thoroughness on the detective's part but might also cloud the issue. Sometimes, the principal clue – which in this case was a motive that pointed to the killer – stood in plain sight but had gone undetected. And since he didn't have access to the official evidence, he tried to deduce an answer from the bits and pieces of information he had gathered from various sources.

He was fashioning a bow sprit for his large miniature of the great sailing vessel and wrestling once again with the relatively few things he knew about the Swallow murder when his phone rang. He was tempted not to answer it, but the ring had persistence – made possible by his disconnected answering machine – that suggested a matter of importance. "Yeah," he said at last into the receiver, still not convinced his response was warranted.

"Hi, Bill, this is Andy Masterson," Andy Masterson announced.

"Son of a gun," Price exclaimed in mild relief. He had almost expected a marketing call or a solicitation from some boiler room operation trying to extract money for the beleaguered families of dead police officers or firefighters. "What brings you to town?"

"I'm not in town, at least not now," Masterson said, and went on to explain he would be there within a few days, implying the trip was part of an ongoing FBI investigation. He failed to reveal, however, his undercover mob assignment and that the visit had been ordered by his crime boss, Dom Chino, through his principal enforcer, Ivor McCusky, who had tried and failed to kill Frank Baines on the very day someone else carried out the deed. All of this, of course, was unknown to Price when Andy Masterson, an FBI agent assigned to an eastern field office and the natural son of his dead lover, Diana Hornbeck, made what otherwise would have been a routine inquiry. "Do you know a man named Timothy Swallow?"

"I knew Tim Swallow," Price replied, correcting his tense and wondering what in hell an east coast FBI agent had to do with the local mess.

Chapter Twelve

As head waiter at The Bristol Bar and Grill for many years, Aldo Carnavali had deferred to a variety of affluent patrons who, more often than not, earned less than he did and fell short of his considerable social polish. Aldo carefully retained his Italian accent with the understanding it was an essential part of the suave image he had cultivated along with impeccable public manners and the cosmopolitan bearing that had made him particularly popular with many women customers. Away from the dining room, however, Aldo's European charm could occasionally disappear when some server did something he considered unprofessional or stupid. "Crap for brains," he would storm at the offenders in English almost devoid of accent, although the recipients of these outbursts were usually undisturbed by a man they knew as a decent boss who simply held them to high standards.

There was never any need for Aldo to redress Grace Goodson, his long-time lover and the waitress with the most seniority in the dining room. She was entirely competent and the only one on the staff immune to his displeasure, although a sense of discretion and attachment to the man kept her from displaying this power. She never exercised it in the presence of others, but those who knew them understood who ran their private lives. "Gracee," he called her with infinite affection, even on those rare occasions when some disagreement between them had motivated this passionate woman to throw an available household object at him. He had long since learned that she either missed – which meant no harm was done – or inflicted some minor injury she remorsefully set right by screwing him as a form of contrition. A man with his own passions, Aldo came to appreciate these little injuries but did his best to avoid anything that might result in hospitalization or permanent damage.

While not friends in the traditional social sense, Aldo Carnavali and Bill Price had developed a relationship based on those hard to define qualities that enable two people to like one another. They met when Carnavali first arrived on the job, young and inexperienced, and Price was a senior homicide detective as well as an established patron of the restaurant. In time, the waiter assumed responsibility for the section that contained Price's favorite booth, which brought them together with enough frequency to establish, over the years, a curious bond that served both their interests.

For his part, Aldo was meticulous in his attention to Price's dining requirements but, more importantly, he evolved into a regular source of information the detective found both interesting and useful. Aldo never intentionally eavesdropped on his customers, although he absorbed conversational fragments like a sponge in the course of silently attending many of the region's prominent political, business, social and other personalities as they dined at The Bristol, barely aware of his constant presence. Always discrete, the waiter seemed to know those things that would interest the detective, and never bothered him with stories that were merely titillating. He reserved those for quiet moments with Grace, who was amused by the foibles of those she often served with carefully hidden distain.

There had never been a reciprocal agreement of any kind, but Price repaid Aldo with minor favors, including his intercession with police when one of his domestic disputes with Grace got out of hand or when his driving, never very good, resulted in some traffic incident. He also advised the waiter on certain financial matters, mainly suggestions to avoid fast-talking promoters who peddled a variety of investment schemes the detective knew were too good to be true. Instead, he directed Aldo to more prudent options that eventually made him, if not actually wealthy, quite comfortable and even more grateful to his long-standing benefactor.

"Mr. Price," Aldo said to Price early one evening at The Bristol. "There's something that might interest you." The detective had abandoned his efforts to get him to use his first name, a practice that seemed entirely too familiar for the old world sensibilities of the head waiter.

'I wouldn't be surprised," Price replied. "What's up?" They had met just inside the dining room, which at that hour was still empty of the crowd that would soon gather.

"There were two men here for lunch on the day Mr. Swallow was killed," he began and went on to explain they were strangers, one with a pronounced east coast accent and a secretive manner. The other man was expensively dressed and more talkative, he recalled. Aldo, Price knew, had a keen ear for dialect, even in English, and an eye for detail. Their presence in itself was not particularly suspicious, the waiter continued, but he overheard one of them use Floyd Sparrow's name and then point to Tim Swallow as that brother passed some distance from their table. "I think one man was identifying Mr. Floyd for the other man, and got the two mixed up," Aldo concluded. He hadn't mentioned the incident to the police because it occurred while he was occupied with work and only marginally aware of the events, which slowly emerged into his consciousness some time later.

Price extracted a description of the two men for his own purposes and advised Aldo to pass the information on to the lead detective, Gunther Hagle. He then thanked him and inquired about the menu specials for the evening.

"I think the grilled pickerel is quite good," Aldo informed him, personally preferring the rack of lamb but aware his aging client ate more fish these days in an effort to preserve, as the old cop put it, what was left of his health. He also heard Price say he carefully alternated his diet between fresh water and ocean fish to ensure a balance between different toxins, mainly the polychlorinated biphenyls and mercury that had famously contaminated fisheries around the world. Aldo didn't get the joke and would not have been amused had he understood it.

111

Although Marvin Sylvester had previously dined at The Bristol, he was not a regular customer and Aldo Carnavali had not seen him before he overheard the conversation that eventually aroused his suspicion. But Aldo's description of him to Hagle was so specific the detective was able to connect the image to one of his suspects and confirm the identification with a photograph. "That's him," Aldo said without hesitation the moment he was confronted with Sylvester's picture. His companion, however, defied identification, although Hagle, based on his informant's description of the man's accent, manner and his presence on the day Tim Swallow was murdered, thought him worthy of some suspicion.

That suspicion was intensified when Hagle interrogated Sylvester, who claimed he didn't recall either the lunch or his companion on the particular day Aldo had seen him in the restaurant. "I eat with someone almost every day of the week," the suspect explained, "and I don't remember most of the people or where we had lunch." He said he was more likely to remember what he had eaten than who he had eaten with unless the meal had produced additional business for his company. "What's this all about, anyway?" he asked with dead certainty it had something to do with the Swallow murder that by this time was common knowledge, particularly to anyone who was remotely familiar with the recent history of The Bristol Bar and Grill.

"It's part of an ongoing investigation," Hagle replied. He did not disclose his knowledge of the concrete contractor's affair with Mona Swallow or his failure to believe Sylvester did not remember either the lunch or his companion on a day that was not that distant in time. He noted, too, that the man, despite his apparent slickness, seemed a bit fidgety, which added to his conviction he had something to hide. The interrogation produced nothing in the way of tangible evidence, but it increased Hagle's certainty there was some connection between the stranger who had lunched with Sylvester and the murder later that day.

For his part, Sylvester had his own suspicions. He suspected Hagle did not believe his failure to recall the lunch or the identity of the stranger who had been with him. This inkling gave him a feeling of unease, which probably would have been more pronounced had Hagle

112

told him his misidentification of Tim Swallow had been overheard. Still, he had been drawn into the investigation, and there was nothing from his point of view that could be done about it.

Hagle subsequently interviewed the Swallow wives, Mona and the new widow, Mimi, whose candor surprised him. "I'm sorry Tim's dead," she told him directly, "but I'm not particularly grief-stricken." She went on to recount his infidelity with Mona and without intention revealed to the detective she was unaware of his many couplings with various woman at the restaurant. Hagle was inclined to believe her ignorance in that regard, but also realized it might have been feigned to lessen any motive she might have had for murdering her duplicitous husband.

She also told him about the phone call that disclosed her husband's affair with his sister-in-law, and looked the cop in the eye when she denied any part in the crime. "I wanted only a divorce and proper maintenance for the children," Mimi said. She didn't bother to tell him she had inherited family wealth, another piece of information he would receive later from Bill Price.

In Hagle's meeting with Mona Swallow, he soon learned her capacity for deception had not been exaggerated by any of his earlier findings. She lied when he asked if she knew Sylvester, and pretended her relations with the late Tim Swallow had been entirely familial and not particularly close. Hagle had the impression she tried to portray herself as the loyal wife, pretending support for her husband but implying at the same time he had motive for the murder. The motive she suggested in a round-about way was control of The Bristol Bar and Grill.

Of the two wives, Mona seemed easily the more devious and the one most likely to have some kind of involvement in the crime. But Hagle knew from long experience as well as inherent common sense that superficial appearances could be deceptive. He understood that Mimi was probably a better person in the moral and social sense than Mona, but he also realized that murders are committed by all kinds of people for a wide variety of reasons. With that knowledge, he reserved judgment of the two women pending the accumulation of more evidence.

Hagle's increasing trust in Price's judgment and discretion, which after a while was reciprocated, developed into a form of collaboration that was so natural neither of them noticed it had happened. They formed a bond based mainly on their mutual interest in the case, but supported by an unspoken respect for one another. Working together – one in an official capacity and the other for the hell of it – they were eventually able to identify the east coast stranger who had lunched with Sylvester on the day of the murder. Price provided the initial clue based on information he got from Andrew Masterson, and Hagle confirmed their initial suspicions with hard evidence from a variety of sources.

Andy Masterson had called Price when he learned the death of Frank Baines had not ended the murderous connection between their two cities. He discovered another assassin – from a mob other than the one he had infiltrated – had been dispatched ahead of Ivor McCusky to kill the exiled thug. "The word around here is that a prominent local citizen was behind the whole thing," he told Price.

"And who's the citizen?" Price inquired, almost certain he knew the answer, which accounted for his lack of surprise when his friend identified Desmond Black and explained the man's motive. Unaware Price had contacted Black in an effort to get him to use whatever influence he had – up to and including lethal force – Masterson sought to warn him that the real killer might have a secondary target, perhaps someone at The Bristol Bar and Grill. He didn't reveal he had overheard more conversations between his mob boss, Dom Chino, and a variety of large and small time criminals as they lunched or dined at Figaro's Trottoria. As a result, he had pieced together information that linked the killer to Pete Huggins, who in all probability had made the arrangements for his law client, Desmond Black.

Masterson had combined fragments of these conversations with reams of background material the FBI had assembled on the local mobs to reach conclusions he passed on to Price. The field agent had come to mistrust the judgment of his immediate superior, and thought the retired cop – who had connections with the local police and at The Bristol - was more likely to achieve results than anything done through

114

official channels. "Maybe we can prevent a second murder," he observed.

"Too late," Price said, and told him about Tim Swallow's death. He also told him about his suspicion the two men had been killed with the same gun, which now seemed a reasonable probability. The probability would become a certainty a few days later when the ballistics report confirmed the slugs removed from both Frank Baines and Tim Swallow came from the same .45 caliber weapon. But, meanwhile, Price wanted to know if Masterson could identify the man sent west to commit two separate murders.

" I'd bet on a character named Paul Small, who they call Little Paulie," Masterson said, explaining his opinion was based only on widespread rumor in the criminal community and not on first-hand knowledge. "The guy's not five feet seven but he's built like a tank and, judging by his reputation, is almost as deadly," he added. " Little Paulie works for one of the local mobs, but he's been known to freelance."

" Do you think Little Paulie could have come here to scratch Baines for one client, and gone on to kill Swallow for someone else? " Price asked, aware he was as likely to know the answer as Masterson.

" It's possible," his friend replied. " These people like to work away from their home turf, where dead bodies attract attention to other activities."

" I' ll pass Little Paulie's name along to the detective on the case, but I'll keep you out of it," Price said. If the killer's identification proved accurate, he thought Hagle might be able to pressure the nervous Sylvester into disclosing whatever he knew about the death of Tim Swallow. More specifically, he wanted to know who had commissioned the crime, and was certain Desmond Black, who was probably behind the assassination of Frank Baines, had nothing to do with the second killing. Price was not inclined to involve Black, whose only daughter had been beaten to death by Baines and whose own death in that hotel corridor seemed a classic case of justifiable homicide to the old cop. And while he hadn't been particularly fond of Tim Swallow, he considered the murder of someone prominently connected to The Bristol as a personal affront. There was also a sustained gnawing sensation in his stomach when matters of that sort went unresolved.

"Any chance you'll visit us any time soon?" Price asked the FBI agent during the declining moments of their conversation. He had decided to pass the residue of Diana Hornbeck's estate on to her son, but wanted to explain the matter face to face.

"There is," Masterson replied. "I can't set a date yet, but I'll let you know well ahead of my arrival." He had thought about revisiting Price, mainly to renew the discussion about his mother. But his insinuation into the Chino mob had put him in a delicate position, and he had to devise an iron-clad excuse for any time he spent away from a boss who had survived mainly as a result of his inordinate suspicions. All this, of course, was unknown to Price, who thought Masterson was simply overloaded with case work as he had often been during his years on the force.

"I think Little Paulie is the mysterious stranger who had lunch with Sylvester on the day Tim Swallow got greased," Hagle later told Price, who had passed the information along to him shortly after his conversation with Andy Masterson. The detective had subsequently built a rather substantial file on the suspect based mainly on sketchy police profiles from his home city as well as airline and taxi records that put him in town and at The Bristol on the day of the murder. Aldo Carnavali, once he saw the police photograph Hagle showed him, put Little Paulie at the table with Sylvester. "He had the Arctic Char," Aldo recalled. "It was on special that day."

Given the accumulated evidence, which Hagle exaggerated, the detective finally got Sylvester to admit he had lunched that day with Little Paulie, although he claimed to know him only as Mr. Small who sought him out with some vague construction project. The exact nature of that enterprise, however, eluded the concrete contractor, whose evasions only served to further implicate him in the Swallow murder. As his questions took on a more accusatory tone, Hagle sensed the man's reluctance to fully acknowledge his association with the out-of-town mobster went beyond his own implication in the

116

homicide. His fear of Little Paulie was palpable and Hagle recognized it for what it was. Given his choice between a murder conviction in a state that had no capital punishment and the wrath of an accomplished killer, Sylvester's choice was, for him, an easy one. After demanding access to his lawyer, he retreated into a profound silence that lasted until Hagle released him with the notice they had not seen the last of one another.

Later, in what Hagle called a "classically stupid" attempt to sort out their accumulating problems, Sylvester met Mona Swallow at a small, out-of-the-way lounge, where they had what the detective who followed them described as a "worried looking" conversation over several cocktails. "These people," Hagle observed to Price the next day, "are probably too dumb to commit murder."

"On the contrary," Price replied, "they're probably just dumb enough."

Chapter Thirteen

"Son of a bitch," Little Paulie muttered to the lifeless body that lay in a crumpled heap before him. "I'd strangle you again if I could." He had killed the man with his bare hands, but the victim – who wore no underwear – had in his death struggle peed down a pant leg and onto one of Paulie's shoes. The killer would years later remember this event, much as others recall their first sexual experience or some other pivotal moment. And while the brutality of his act eluded him, the humor attached to the recollection did not.

Paulie had murdered the man for personal reasons and not for money, but the ease of its execution and the failure of authorities to exact any punishment set him on a path that eventually made him a killer for hire. He was not particularly blood-thirsty and took no pleasure in murder, but he had a knack for the work and the pay was good.

Little Paulie eventually developed an underworld reputation as a cold, efficient executioner, a persistent and remorseless assassin whose services were prized by the crime bosses who mainly employed him. Born Paul Oliver Small, the Little Paulie nickname – which he despised – was attached to him in recognition of his enormous density. That size was figured in cubic volume rather than height, where he fell a few inches short of the norm. Paulie had a low center of gravity and sufficient bulk to give him great natural strength, apparent in a short, massive neck that made his head appear smaller than the reality.

Both his reputation and appearance inspired respect and deference among the diverse group of criminals who either knew him personally or knew about him. Unlike some who killed others for a living, he neither sought nor bothered about anonymity.

Although he had surely murdered his share of men – mostly criminals in their own right who had run afoul of some rival or gang, but never women or children – he had been credited with far more deaths than any one person could have accumulated in a busy lifetime. Many of the rumors and stories that attached to him were mostly false, but there was enough truth to explain the phenomenon. Paulie was aware of this situation, and mostly amused by it. He also understood the inspiration of fear was useful in his line of work.

Paul Small had more than sufficient intelligence to recognize that and other kinds of advantages, which he employed in developing his offbeat career. He was, in fact, often smarter than the men who hired him and was careful to accept only those jobs he could manage in terms of risk. Paulie knew his work was dangerous, but thought with reasonable prudence he could survive into relative old age and a comfortable retirement in some secluded, balmy place. He was even smart enough to know that was an optimistic assumption.

The youngest child in a family of seven with three older brothers and an equal number of sisters, Paul grew up in a lower middle class suburb where there had been few, if any, environmental factors to explain the homicidal direction his life would eventually take. His parents were decent enough, but somewhat distant given the need to spread their attention over so many children in the relatively few hours they were not working modest-salaried jobs. That circumstance gave him, perhaps, more independence at an early age than he needed, and deprived him of the discipline that, given his intelligence, would have made him a more diligent student. Instead, he began early in his teen years to regularly skip school, which bored him, and to spend time in the nearby city where he discovered a variety of more interesting venues. His two favorites were Bucky's Billiards, which was mostly a pool hall, and a whore house that catered mainly to small time hoodlums, gamblers and other assorted riffraff. At 14 or 15, Paulie saw this collection of losers in a light made positive by their abilities to avoid hard work and other societal obligations which, to him, had ruined the lives of his industrious parents.

"Sugar," was the name applied to him by Miss Clemmens, the hardboiled madam, then in her early 50s, who ran the whore house with a degree of discipline not often seen outside a maximum security prison. She had developed something beyond fondness for the boy, who originally appeared at her back door pretending to seek work of some kind but really interested in gaining access to a place he assumed was full of naked women. His little artifice didn't fool the wily madam, who was amused by his attempted deception and attracted to this sturdy kid who looked several years older than his true age. As it turned out, she had a natural inclination toward very young men and Paulie appeared at a time when the demands of her business were lighter than usual. As a consequence, she took his virginity that same day and gained a degree of gratitude from him that was evident several weeks later.

"I want my money or I'll take it out of your wrinkled hide," a large, florid-faced man demanded of Miss Clemmens as Paulie arrived at the house early one afternoon. He had entered through the kitchen door and found the two engaged in a heated argument. "I may take it out of your hide, anyway," the man said and grasped her neck with both of his big hands. She tried simultaneously to knee his groin and scratch his face with her sharp fingernails, but he held her at sufficient distance to thwart those efforts. She was gasping for breath and had recognized her desperate situation when she heard a loud, dull thud and her assailant instantly released his powerful grip and dropped to the floor, either unconscious or dead.

"Jesus Christ," she gasped, dropping to her knees next to the inert body and looking up at Paulie, who stood there with a large, iron skillet in his hand. He had dropped her assailant with a single blow to the back of his shaved head from a weapon he found on the nearby stove.

"Are you okay?" he inquired.

Paulie had not killed the man, who regained consciousness an hour later in a distant, rat-infested alley where a couple of the madam's associates had unceremoniously dumped him. He had no idea what had put him in that position and no inclination to again confront the woman who had apparently done it. She, meanwhile, showed her appreciation to Paulie in ways he had not even suspected, and later had her cook feed him enough to restore his depleted energies.

This teenager who looked more like a young man also became something of a fixture at the rundown pool hall, Bucky's Billiards, where he initially did chores and ran errands for the owner, Buckminster O'Malley, and eventually developed enough skill at Eight Ball to hustle the odd stranger. Long divorced and without children, Bucky – who was in his early 60s but looked a decade older as the result of a hard-drinking life – liked Paulie and came to depend on his energy and strength to do those things he was either not inclined or in some cases unable to do himself.

Bucky's Billiards was a dusty old place with a random assortment of worn pool tables lit by green shaded lights that hung from the high ceiling. There was also the single billiard table that gave the place its name, and a small bar where only domestic beer and a modest selection of cheap liquors were dispensed along with chips, pickled sausage and jerky by either Bucky himself or one of his itinerant employees. Despite its dinginess, Bucky's or Buck's as it was known to the regulars, was seldom empty or closed. The long hours were sustained despite state laws that regulated such matters and which suggested Bucky paid someone for the privilege.

As Paulie's teen years passed, he gathered strength and responsibilities at the pool hall where he eventually took on an unofficial manager's role. Bucky was not one to bestow titles, but the young man came to handle everything from the reported business receipts – which were only a fraction of the various transactions done at the place – to the ejection of bothersome drunks and other troublemakers. Given the latter chore, Bucky supplied Paulie with a small revolver, assuming it would only be used to intimidate those who were unresponsive to lesser threats. He was dead wrong on that score.

"What in hell were you thinking?" Bucky demanded of Paulie, who late one night shot a particularly mean drunk in the leg to make his point. Bucky had no sympathy for the drunk, but didn't want to call police attention to a business that skirted the law in many respects.

"The bastard asked for it," Paulie replied. "He's lucky I didn't shoot him where it really hurts." He didn't tell his boss he could have thrown the drunk out with little difficulty, but elected to shoot him in some non-critical body part to make a statement. He figured word of the event would get around the neighborhood, and make his job easier in the long run. The intention showed early evidence of strategic thinking, but this virtue – even had he recognized it – was lost on Buckminster O'Malley. He fired Paulie straight away and gave the shooting victim a thousand dollars to forget the whole thing which, considering he barely remembered it, he did with something approaching gratitude.

For his part, Paulie took his firing personally, and heaved a heavy bar stool thorough the big plate glass window that fronted the pool hall, sending large shards down on the sidewalk and raining lesser bits in various directions. "Report this to the cops," he told his former mentor, "and I'll come back and shoot you, too." Bucky took the threat to heart and never saw the young man again.

The episode was witnessed by some of Bucky's customers, who soon made it a matter of general conversation throughout the local underworld community. Most of those who either witnessed the event or heard the story thought it funny, although one of the mob bosses – a shrewd survivor named Zeno Magruder – had an entirely different take on the aggressive young man. He detected certain useful qualities and thought Paulie might serve some purpose in his organization. Magruder subsequently hired him as something like an apprentice thug assigned to do things his veteran goons would not have happily done. He ran errands, answered phones and stood around the saloon, Kiley's, which his new boss owned and used as a combination social hall and base of operations. In that city, any boss who aspired to a respectable career in criminal management had to own a bar or restaurant

By this time, Paulie – who had left home several years earlier -

had a small, furnished apartment and appreciation for his independence. Oddly, perhaps, for someone who hated formal education and had dropped out of high school early, he developed an intense interest in books and read widely on subjects as varied as the firearms he soon learned to expertly use to military history. He was particularly interested in Napoleon Bonaparte, impressed with the disparity between his small size and towering achievements.

"What's that?" one of Magruder's thugs asked Paulie in reference to the book he was reading in the back room at Kiley's during a lunch break. There was no reply, but it was apparent from Paulie's silence and the expression on his face that he thought the question was stupid.

"You snotty little bastard," the man thought but kept it to himself. He and most of the others in the gang were reluctant to confront this newcomer, who had no stature in the organization but whose manner told them he was strangely different from the rest. They also knew about the trouble at Bucky's and would soon learn, mostly through rumor, that he had carried out a murder for Magruder, who had come to recognize Paulie's aptitude for that kind of work. He killed a small-time drug dealer who tried to sever ties with Magruder and go into business for himself, an error in judgment that cost him his life and put Paulie on a new career path.

"You got the job done, but there was no need to empty your piece into the poor slob," Magruder told him later. "One well-placed slug would have sent the same message." Paulie, who had assumed a bullet-riddled body made a strong statement, realized the advice made sense and from then on his assassinations, with few exceptions, were models of tidiness. One of the exceptions, however, was a near giant, Big Melvin Malloy, who absorbed a full clip of small caliber ammunition, including two shots to the head and one to the heart, before he finally went down and convinced Paulie a more substantial weapon could have averted the problem. Afterward, he adopted a .45 caliber auto pistol, which provided reasonable assurance his victims would not hang around to complicate his life. There were, of course, situations that required more than a single shot to ensure the target had been dispatched to eternity rather than to some nearby hospital. And there were occasions, too, when a gun was inappropriate for one reason or another, and other weapons - knives, garrotes and Paulie's own bare hands – were employed to deplete the criminal population in a number of cities in this country and across both borders.

Paulie's natural strength and native abilities were considerable, but he also honed his skills through conscientious practice with all the weapons in his arsenal. He became an expert in the use and maintenance of handguns, various kinds of knives and other instruments that could be applied to killing someone at close distance. He took little interest in long guns of any type under the assumption a shot from afar left too much to chance.

As Paulie perfected his craft and gained a reputation for reliability, Magruder farmed his services out to other mob bosses and cut himself in for a percentage of the take. He began to see his killer for hire in much the same way the chief executive of a large parent corporation might view a very profitable subsidiary. Little Paulie became something of a cash cow for his mob, and also enabled Magruder to establish business links with other criminal organizations. Eventually, too, he allowed Paulie to negotiate his own independent contracts with the provision he receive a reasonable cut and there were no conflicts with his interests, business or personal.

Magruder had no fear of Paulie, but was smart enough to treat the young man with respect, aware he had a short fuse and the demonstrated capacity for murder. For his part, Paulie saw his boss as an agent, someone who handled the details and gave him time to develop his skills and do the real work. It was a mutually satisfactory arrangement that would eventually put this trained killer in the hotel corridor where Dandy Frank Baines drew his last breath and behind The Bristol Bar and Grill on the evening Tim Swallow was shot. But Paulie was only the instrument and not the instigator of these murders, and had no feelings one way or the other about his victims. Other than women and children, they were all the same to him with one exception.

Over time and as he improved his lethal skills, Paulie came to take increasing pride in his work and to have little tolerance for anything or anyone that caused him to bungle a job. And since he had mistakenly shot Tim Swallow instead of his brother, Floyd, at the specific direction of Marvin Sylvester, he held the nervous concrete contractor accountable for the mistake. "I'm going to whack that stupid son-of-a-bitch," Paulie told Magruder when he learned of the error.

"Forget it," Magruder advised him under the assumption he had sense enough to drop the matter. He had been paid well for the job and Sylvester and whoever had put him up to the killing were now trying to distance themselves from the deed. They had no interest in another murder as they tried to avoid implication in the original one. Paulie, however, was driven by his own demented logic, which told him to complete the original job, which was to kill Floyd Swallow, and to also exact revenge on the man who had caused him to botch the assignment. He had no idea a detective named Hagle had tied him to both murders or he would have abandoned what soon became an absolute intention. His logic was twisted in some ways, but reasonably sound in others.

"I'm going to take a few days off," Paulie told Magruder, who thought a little time away from Kiley's, where he mainly killed time rather than someone, was a good idea. He had no notion Paulie had booked a flight west with plans to scout his two victims and then shoot them dead at the first prudent opportunity. Had he known, he would have put a contract out on Paulie, whose rashness would have been entirely unacceptable to this very practical crook.

Chapter Fourteen

"I quit the FBI," Andrew Masterson told Bill Price shortly after they had been seated for lunch at The Bristol Bar and Grill.

"That is a surprise," Price replied. "I figured you for a career with those guys." Actually, he was not surprised, although the exact nature of the news was unexpected. He knew something out of the ordinary had happened to his friend, alerted by his sudden appearance in town without an earlier phone call.

"My boss put me in an untenable position, one that was both stupid and dangerous," Masterson explained without really telling him anything. "He left me with no alternative, at least none that made any sense."

"What now?" Price inquired under the assumption the younger man would explain more about the resignation if that was his inclination.

"I'm not sure, but the idea of something in a warm climate would suit me just fine," he said. "I've had preliminary thoughts about the British Virgin Islands or Costa Rica."

"I don't think the law enforcement agencies in those places are recruiting many Yankees," Price observed.

"I don't plan to enforce any laws," he replied. "In fact, I don't know what I want to do. I've decided to first figure out where I want to do it." He explained the geography of his life had previously been determined by his work and that he wanted to reverse that process. "I want to settle in some really good place."

"I might be able to make your transition to civilian life a little easier," Price said and then told him about Diana Hornbeck's estate and his decision to pass it on to him as her son and to his knowledge only surviving relative. The older man watched his friend digest the information, which was completely at odds with the thoughts that had consumed him.

"I couldn't take the money," he said at last. "It was meant for you."

"Sure you could and no it wasn't," Price responded with something akin to amusement. "She would want you to have it and I don't need it." As far as he was concerned, that settled the matter. Not yet convinced, Masterson needed time to consider the offer, which he would eventually accept with both gratitude and the realization it couldn't have come at a better time. He had left his job out of absolute necessity and with few resources or prospects for immediate new employment. And there was the possibility an angry mob boss either had or would soon put out a contract on his life.

Masterson had not disclosed his undercover work to Price, and was even more reluctant to tell him about the chain of events that led to his present predicament. There had been a leak of some kind and the underboss, Ivor McCusky, learned someone, presumably for an agency of law enforcement, had been planted in the gang. He didn't know for certain that Andy Masterson was the mole, but his general background and newness to the organization put him under immediate suspicion. In McCusky's cold analysis of the situation, that suspicion was tantamount to absolute guilt.

"Albert," McCusky said to Big Al Moroski one afternoon when he had dispatched Masterson on an errand, "our young friend may be working for someone else and I need you to take care of the situation." Big Al was no genius, but he understood his boss perfectly and would have killed Masterson at the first opportunity had the FBI agent not realized his cover had been blown. As usual, he had put the information together from bits and pieces of conversation he overheard and from his perceptive interpretation of nuances in the way he was treated by McCusky and Moroski, who was his immediate superior in the gang.

128

Masterson told the special agent in charge of his FBI field office, his real boss, about the situation, and asked his permission to evacuate the undercover assignment as soon as possible. "They're on to me, and that's a death sentence if I don't bail out," he had said. But Masterson's inside information on the mob had been useful, and the agent in charge wanted him to remain undercover for a bit longer, just enough time to complete an investigation that seemed promising. Masterson agreed, unaware he had far less time than even he had guessed before McCusky tried, through Big Al, to kill him.

"Let's take a trip," Al had said to Masterson, which was his usual way of telling the younger man they had received some kind of assignment from McCusky. But Al's manner was different in some inexplicable way and he asked Masterson to drive, which was contrary to his usual practice and suggested to the agent that the journey, at least for one of them, would not be roundtrip.

"What's the deal?" Masterson inquired as they drove away from Kiley's in a direction Al had indicated with a hand gesture. "We're goin' to Pottsville," he said, which indicated a small town some distance from the city where the organization maintained a small warehouse.

"I'd better get some gas," Andy Masterson, who was known in the mob as Andy Anderson, said, and then drove until he reached an outlying service station that at the moment was completely devoid of customers. "You need anything from inside?" he asked and parked the car at a pump equally obscured from the cashier's window and the highway.

"Nope," Big Al replied, unaware it would be his last response. Masterson got out of the car, circled it and with his pistol put a single shot into the temple of his would-be killer's head through the open window on the passenger side. Al's body jerked away from the shot, but Masterson pulled him back into an upright position before he quickly left the station for a bus stop he knew was only two short blocks away. The corpse remained that way for several hours before it fell over and was accidentally discovered by someone more attentive than the cashier.

As Masterson rode the bus back to the city and his own car, he realized Ivor McCusky would soon know what had happened and would surely be after him with all the criminal resources at his disposal. Given that inevitability, he decided to kill McCusky if he could, aware the mob boss, Dom Chino, would be temporarily at a loss to replace his principal enforcer. This dangerous task, Masterson soon learned, proved far easier than he had expected.

The underboss had survived a number of attempts on his life, some in the state penitentiary where he had done time and run a gang of murderous thugs to the tough city streets that had made him what he was. Like others of his kind, he was compulsively watchful and trusted no one, but Masterson understood that his greatest strength, fearlessness, was, perhaps, his main weakness. McCusky had the notion he could take care of himself and often moved about the city, heavily armed but alone.

"Hello, Mac," Masterson said to McCusky. "Big Al sends his regards." He was in the back seat of McCusky's late model Cadillac – which was parked that night behind Figaro's Trottoria - with his gun pressed against the back of the gangster's skull.

"Yeah," McCusky replied, "how is Big Al?"

"Dead," Masterson informed him and discharged a single slug into his head, the sound muffled to the outside world by acoustic measures that made many modern automobiles relatively soundproof. He had broken into the car and waited for almost an hour for McCusky, who died instantly from a bullet that traversed his brain and finally lodged in the dashboard.

The next day, Masterson submitted his resignation to his FBI superior by phone with no explanation and without the invitation to kiss his ass that was present in his thoughts. He felt the man's ambition to rise in the organization over his dead body was justification for a comment of that nature, but he kept it to himself. He figured there would be some mystery attached to the killings of the two gangsters, McCusky and Big Al, and he was content to let the man ponder those events and the connection to his resignation. "Chew on that," he had thought as he packed a single bag and left his small, furnished apartment for the last time, bound for the airport and a trip to see Bill

Price. The recent events for reasons that eluded him had evoked thoughts of his birth mother, Diana Hornbeck, and he was anxious to talk with the one living person who had been close to her.

There was much that Price didn't know about Diana, who rarely spoke of her life before they met, but he was able to paint an affectionate verbal portrait of the woman as he and Andy Masterson lingered in the booth at The Bristol Bar and Grill. His recollections were a series of anecdotes that reflected her singular personality and brought the woman to life in a way that a more informed recitation of biographical fact never could have done.

"We met in this very restaurant and got off to a rocky start," Price recalled. "She had dumped some obnoxious bastard who took her out and got drunk at one of the dining room tables." He further explained that she went to the bar to escape the man, who followed and was even more annoying until Price, seated nearby, intervened and sent him on his way.

"I thought I'd done her a service, but she was really pissed off," Price continued. "She told me in no uncertain terms she could have handled the situation on her own, and that I should get lost, which I did." He returned to his barstool and sat there alone for about 20 minutes before Diana reconsidered his motives and sent him a conciliatory drink. "We were pals from then on," he said.

Price, of course, would not tell Masterson about their sexual closeness, which had often sponsored some of Diana's saltier comments and the ones that revealed a good deal about her character. "Kiss me, you fool" were the words that revealed she was amenable to sex, which the woman apparently enjoyed but never mistook for anything other than a good time. Although he never bothered to analyze his feelings about sex – which was a regular aspect of his long relationship with Diana – Price, after her death, could not achieve a similar interest in another woman. They buried his libido with Diana and he simply forgot about the phenomenon despite the reminders he got from his horny old friend, Jack McCurdy, who continued to screw any woman who looked at him more than once.

"I think you should know I killed two mob guys several days ago,"

Masterson admitted during a lull in their conversation, which had become more of a prolonged reflection by Price on the life and times of Diana Hornbeck.

"I assume you're okay or we wouldn't be having this conversation," Price replied. He also assumed Masterson had simply dispatched a couple of criminals in the line of duty.

"You don't understand," the younger man began and then explained the general nature of what he had done. He didn't go into detail but told Price about the undercover assignment and his blown cover, which had put him in a precarious situation. His sudden confession had been prompted by a combination of obligation to Price – who had resurrected his mother and was going to pass her estate on to him – and residual guilt related to the murders he had committed. He knew McCusky and Big Al were bad men, but he had been taught during his formative years that killing was not a good way to resolve problems.

"I would have done exactly the same thing," Price told him, aware the confession implied that Masterson was struggling with his conscience. "But," he added, I may not be the best person to judge these matters." He went on to explain he had taken the law into his own hands on several occasions over a long career, although he kept the details to himself. "I not only think the instinct for self-preservation is both strong and reasonable, but I also believe there are people who need killing," he said. "You did the world a favor."

"Maybe," Masterson replied, not convinced, but relieved he had gotten the matter off his chest. The two men sat in silence for a while until Price resumed his reflections on Diana Hornbeck. "She carved the best lemon twist that ever graced vodka on the rocks," he observed at last, neither aware nor concerned the skill meant little to anyone, including Andy Masterson. He was also unaware his real meaning was downright Freudian, given the close association between alcohol and sex in his relationship with Diana. Their drinks together had prompted intimate conversation, which had been the real trigger for physical intimacy.

Later and after Price had arranged a meeting with Masterson the following day to transfer proceeds from Diana's estate, the two men went their separate ways. The younger man had politely declined an invitation to spend the night at Price's apartment, preferring not only to be alone but to remain as anonymous as possible until he had put considerable distance between himself and the mob that would surely try to seek him out. Price, too, was relieved that Masterson had not taken him up on the invitation. He was ill-equipped for guests, mostly because his second bedroom had been given over to his books and work on the various models of the great warship, Victory. Even his living room couch – which would have served as a guest bed – was laden with magazines and other stuff he had set aside for later reference or disposal. The thought of moving all that junk, finding spare sheets and playing host was a prospect he didn't enjoy, but would have endured for his young friend.

Relieved of the obligation, Price worked that evening on his latest model of HMS Victory's figure-head, an emblem mounted on the ship's bow that showed two cupids supporting the British coat of arms surrounded with the royal crown and a motto, in Latin, that announced: "Shame to him who evil thinks." Price thought the motto a bit silly, but had substantial respect for the ship itself and the men who had sailed it into battle.

Admiral Lord Nelson's flagship, he knew, is the oldest commissioned warship in the world and the only surviving vessel that fought in the American and French revolutions as well as the Napoleonic wars. She has a permanent berth at Portsmouth naval base in England, which Price had long meant to visit. Victory is an 18th century first-rate warship on which construction was begun in 1759, some 47 years before Vice Admiral Horatio Lord Nelson defeated the French fleet at Trafalgar in one of the most decisive naval battles, both tactically and strategically, in history.

Price understood that HMS Victory was essentially a floating gun platform that delivered devastating broadsides from its powerful gun batteries, arranged in tiers on three decks. The ship was devised for the strategy of the British royal navy in the days of the old square riggers, which in battle would line up astern of each other and sail in a line past the enemy. The canons, which could not be swiveled, were aimed and fired when the ship was abeam of that enemy, who in all discourtesy returned the fire during a long and deadly passage.

Price often thought of the actual battle at Trafalgar, where Nelson was mortally wounded, as he worked on his various models. Those great wooden warships were incredibly sturdy, but anyone who stood on deck against those withering broadsides faced a hail of deadly shrapnel from enemy canons at relatively close range and equally lethal splinters that flew all about the place. Price – who had faced down hardened criminals and survived a number of life-threatening and other dangerous situations during his years on the force – wondered from time to time how he would have stood up in an 18th or early 19th century naval battle. Nelson – a small man even by the standard of his time – had lost a number of body parts in the course of a seemingly fearless career, which must have made him even more diminutive by the time his death and victory at Trafalgar made him one of England's greatest heros.

"What a guy," Price thought as he worked leisurely on his latest model and pondered the personality of the admiral and the actual construction of the real vessel, which took over 5000 carefully selected mature oak trees to build along with elm, pine and fir which had to be seasoned for several years. These and a multitude of other accumulated facts flowed through his thoughts, which included a considerable distain for the ambitious Napoleon whose massive ego had sent his admiral, Villeneuve, to ruinous defeat at Trafalgar. Bonaparte's imperious nature, which brought him to ultimate disaster, reminded Price of a former police commissioner whose personality and fate had been similar, although on a considerably smaller scale. This particular thought was in his mind when the phone rang, an annoyance he almost decided to ignore before answering it against his better judgment. "Yeah," he said into the offending instrument.

"Mr. Price," Aldo Carnavali responded with something that approached excitement. "He's here."

"Who's where?" Price inquired.

"The man with the eastern accent," Aldo explained. "The one who mistook Mr. Tim for Mr. Floyd. He's in the dining room."

134

The possibility Tim Swallow's murderer had returned to the crime scene seemed remote to Price, but he trusted Aldo's unerring memory of those who passed through The Bristol's dining room. "That goon's return," he thought, "can only mean one thing." He reasoned that Little Paulie had come back to finish the original job, which was to kill Floyd Swallow. There seemed no plausible explanation other than a rare mistake on Aldo's part, which seemed even more remote to Price than Paulie's appearance at The Bristol.

"Tell Floyd to lock himself in his office until I get there," he instructed the head waiter, who he also told to go about his business as if nothing unusual was afoot. He then called Hagle to pass on the news, but the detective had temporarily turned off his cell phone. He was attending a birthday party for the five-year-old daughter of a younger friend and had not wanted a call to interrupt the festivities.

"God damn," Price muttered to himself in frustration as he hurriedly dressed and retrieved his gun from a table drawer next to his bed. As an afterthought, he also took the small backup piece, a hammerless, snubnose revolver he wore in an ankle holster but had not used since his retirement. "You never know," he thought as he headed for the front door.

Chapter Fifteen

"Little Paulie killed me," Marvin Sylvester said a bit prematurely to Hagle, his voice barely audible as he lay dying on an EMS gurney outside his apartment building. He and Mona Sparrow had been shot, both stark naked, in his bedroom, but she had died instantly.

"Why?" Hagle inquired, not really expecting an answer and genuinely surprised when he got one.

"It was her idea," he said. "She wanted her husband dead." Sylvester knew he was dying and the words he struggled to discharge amounted, Hagle realized, to a deathbed confession. The detective listened closely and recorded those words on the small notepad he considered more important to his work than the holstered gun on his belt. Sylvester disclosed Mona Sparrow's unsuccessful attempt – using his criminal contacts – to murder the husband she had long deceived, first with his late brother and subsequently with the man who now incriminated her with his final statement. He told Hagle of the botched assassination, which had claimed Tim Sparrow's life instead of the intended victim, Floyd Sparrow, and of Little Paulie's anger at the person he held responsible for the mistake.

"He blamed me for the whole mess," Sylvester said weakly. Paulie had indicated as much before he squeezed off the shots that dispatched Mona and would soon send her lover to wherever she went. But before his departure, he made a final disclosure that came as a complete surprise to the detective. "She put out the contract on that guy who was killed in the Brighton Hotel," Sylvester said with some difficulty and then died before he could be transferred to the waiting ambulance. He meant that Mona had ordered the death of Dandy Frank Baines, too. Her motive, Hagle would later deduce, was simple enough. She did it to protect herself and her children, apparently not confident anyone else was handling the job. He further speculated that Mona had contrived her meeting and subsequent affair with Sylvester under the assumption he had underworld contacts, although Hagle conceded, given her final naked aspect, that sex had also been a motivating force in the plan. Otherwise, there would have been no need for her to continue the relationship with Sylvester, particularly since the botched effort to kill Floyd Sparrow made a further attempt too risky.

As it turned out, Mona would have survived Sylvester had she not been in bed with him when Little Paulie came to call. The killer had no notion of her involvement and only shot the woman to eliminate a witness. And Sylvester survived long enough to confess only because the two shots he took to the chest put him flat on his back and simulated the corpse he would soon become. In all probability, Paulie would have paid closer attention to him had Mona's presence not complicated the matter. He was not in the habit of killing women, and the obvious need to remove a witness created something of a moral quandary for him. Granted, the quandary only lasted a split second, but it diverted his attention from the main target, Marvin Sylvester.

Although Hagle was reasonably certain the murders had been carried out by Paul Small aka Little Paulie, he would have been surprised to learn the killer had gone directly from Sylvester's apartment to The Bristol Bar and Grill where he had been noticed by the ever vigilant Aldo Carnavali. Paulie, whose appetite was whetted by the recent work, saw no reason not to have dinner as he sought to identify Floyd Sparrow, who he intended to kill on those very premises and end a matter that had been a considerable annoyance to him.

"What's good?" he asked Grace Goodson, his waitress and the love of Aldo Carnavali's life. The coincidence that put Paulie at one of

138

Grace's tables had also been responsible for the promptness with which Aldo had noticed the killer's presence. He kept a close eye on everything in the dining room, but particularly on anything that involved Gracie.

"Everything," she replied, which was her standard response to that standard question. She did, however, go on to describe the special dishes for the day and to make recommendations from the regular menu as Aldo went off to alert Price to Paulie's appearance at the restaurant. He went to Floyd Sparrow's office where he was allowed to use the phone when the restaurant owner was away, as he was that evening and as Aldo had not thought to advise Price during their abbreviated phone conversation.

Floyd Sparrow had decided to divorce Mona and marry June Havens, who was with him in his plane on a flight back to Chicago where they planned a short vacation and where he intended to make a formal marriage proposal. As the Cessna cruised through a clear but darkening sky at 7,000 feet, Floyd, unable to contain his intention, popped the question, unaware a divorce was no longer necessary and that Mona's dead body had been removed from Sylvester's apartment as the authorities tried to contact him with the news. His absence and the rocky nature of his marriage to Mona would have made him a prime suspect had Hagle not known about Little Paulie and the late lovers.

"Is Mr. Sparrow in the restaurant tonight?" Little Paulie asked Grace Goodson when she served the 12 ounce filet he had ordered.

"I wouldn't know," she replied with absolute truth. Grace paid little attention to the movements of anyone not connected with her immediate responsibilities and had no idea Floyd Sparrow was away that evening.

"Who would?" Paulie persisted.

"The head waiter, more than likely," she answered. "I'll ask him when he returns to the dining room." She had noticed Aldo's absence, which was not out of the ordinary. His routine normally took him to many parts of the large establishment, where he was as likely to have business in the kitchen or reception area as he was in the dining room where his seasoned staff preferred he remain out of their collective way.

Paulie thanked her and settled down to enjoy his meal, assuming Floyd Sparrow would be easy enough to find in the restaurant. Marvin Sylvester had told him the Sparrow brothers paid close attention to their business and one of them was always on the premises when the place was open. And since there was only one surviving brother, Paulie drew the conclusion he was surely there and would more than likely show himself before long. That conclusion was the result of plain carelessness, a fault the killer would have formerly found intolerable, but one that now made little difference to him. He had done his lethal work with impunity for so long those earlier precautions seemed unnecessary. He had not even bothered to precisely locate the final victim in his haste to complete the task and return home, all in the same day.

As Paulie chewed on neatly sliced pieces of pink meat, Floyd Sparrow was safely belted into a seat in his plane, two hundred miles away and thousands of feet above the man who sought to murder him. He had told June about the intended divorce, asked her to marry him and gotten a prompt acceptance. Afterward, they sat silently for a while in the darkened cabin, illuminated only by the instrument lights and assured by the steady drone of the plane's single engine they would safely arrive before long at the small airport in the countryside not far from Chicago.

"I've asked Mimi to work at the restaurant," he said to her after a while. "She inherited Tim's share," he added, "but, more importantly, she's smart and I'm convinced she can help run the place."

"Will she do it?" June inquired.

"I think so," Floyd said. "She'll let me know in a week." Floyd went on to explain he wanted someone who could eventually replace his dead brother, someone who could carry half the load that had now been placed on his shoulders. And since Mimi was part owner of the restaurant and was probably up to the task, she seemed to him a logical candidate. "If she accepts, we can break her in together," he continued.

"You make the woman sound like a new Buick," June replied and left unsaid her willingness to do what he had suggested because it wasn't necessary. Floyd knew she liked Mimi, just as he knew she had never liked his wife, the late Mona. And he also suspected her dislike was based on Mona's nasty temperament and had nothing to do with jealousy or less admirable motives. June was the polar opposite of Mona in almost every respect, which was a reassuring thought that passed through Floyd Sparrow's mind as he began the plane's descent toward the airport.

Earlier that day, Mimi Sparrow met Jack McCurdy for lunch and told him about the offer to work at The Bristol. She also told him diplomatically that their physical relationship was over but she hoped they would remain friends.

"Sure," McCurdy replied, aware since it began that the affair – given the great difference in their ages, among other things – would not last long. "And I'm glad you didn't blame yourself."

"I wouldn't do that because it was clearly your fault," she said, going along with his attempt at humor, which barely disguised disappointment.

"My fault?"

"You were born too soon," she explained, wondering whether her remark was a bit insensitive until he provided reassurance to the contrary. He told her he knew they had not been destined for a long term relationship and then changed the subject. "Are you going to take the job?" he asked.

"I think so," she said in a manner that suggested it was almost certain. "I need a change and I'm flattered that Floyd wants me to help out. He could easily have run the restaurant himself and just sent me checks."

As they discussed her future at the restaurant and other things, McCurdy wondered if Mimi had met someone else. She had, but didn't tell him about this development because it was not yet clear it would amount to anything. She wanted, however, to be free of entanglements – even informal ones like McCurdy – in the event something more serious came along with someone who could provide more durable prospects than the horny old policeman who had grown quite fond of her. She was also reluctant to tell him her new lover was a recently divorced, middle-aged gynecologist whose stirrups she had occupied for a number of years but who, out of professional caution and reasonable decency, had made no overtures while they were both married. The doctor finally made a move once his divorce was final and her husband was dead. He asked her out to dinner and declared his long time admiration which, after some thought, she decided was reciprocal. She had the vague notion a doctor closer to her own age was preferable to an old policeman.

Floyd Sparrow learned of his wife's death when he called the restaurant from the airport to make sure there were no problems with the business that someone else couldn't handle. He was momentarily stunned by the news even though he had no conscious feeling for the woman who, he knew, had even less regard for him. As the reality settled in, Floyd realized that Mona's murder – while a tragedy, no doubt, for their children – was a neat solution to his problem. He was free to marry June without a bitter and protracted divorce squabble that would have been burdensome in every respect from emotional to financial.

"What is it?" June asked when he switched off the phone. She was seated next to him in the modest airport lounge, and assumed from the tone of his voice that something had gone wrong.

"Mona's dead," he said, "murdered in some man's bed." He left further explanation for the flight home, which they began immediately after the plane was refueled. As they took off into the night sky, Floyd's thoughts were riddled with ambivalence. He was both relieved and, he soon realized, saddened by Mona's death. Although it had been many years earlier, he had once loved her enough to marry and father two children. And while he still thought of her as the ultimate bitch, he also retained some memory of their few good years together. "Life is a bloody struggle," he thought as the plane gained cruising altitude and he began to tell June what little he knew about the killings.

Bill Price arrived at The Bristol and sought out Aldo Carnavali, who had kept a discrete eye on Little Paulie as he ate dinner and kept his own eye out for the elusive Floyd Sparrow. Paulie had gotten no further information on Sparrow's whereabouts from Grace Goodson, who was busy with other diners. And while he was anxious to identify his target and finish this business, he didn't want his curiosity to attract any more attention than was necessary to get the job done. He decided, consequently, to interrupt his meal for a trip to the men's restroom, which would give him an opportunity to scout the place and, perhaps, find the man whose life he intended to take, but not before he finished dinner.

"Where is this guy?" Price asked Aldo, who had maintained an inconspicuous presence in the dining room at some distance from the table Paulie had occupied only moments earlier.

"I think he went to the men's room," the head waiter speculated with some confidence he was right. "He hasn't finished his dinner and he hasn't ask for a check." The thought a cold-blooded killer might walk out on a check hadn't occurred to him.

"Is Floyd in his office and did you tell him to lock the door?" Price inquired with some urgency. He realized that Sparrow's office and the main restrooms were down the same hall.

"Not to worry," Aldo said. "I forgot to tell you Mr. Floyd is out of town."

Price assimilated the information with some relief, but was left with the sense something had to be done about Little Paulie even if he had to do it himself. He knew Sparrow's absence that evening would only postpone the inevitable attempt on his life. And he also knew his options as an old civilian were far more limited than when he was younger and worked homicides for the city police department.

"What to do?" he thought, but only for a fleeting moment before he gave Hagle's phone number to Aldo and told him to call the detective. "Tell him the killer is here," he said. Price had tried unsuccessfully to phone Hagle on his drive to the restaurant, but thought the waiter might have better luck while he kept track of the evil in their midst. With that in mind, Price went directly to Floyd Swallow's office, where he found the door unlocked and the lights on. As a result of the pressure he felt to watch Paulie, Aldo had not thought to secure the place.

Cautiously and with his hand gripped on his holstered pistol, Price entered the office and found it unoccupied. Suddenly feeling a little wobbly for some reason other than fear, he sat down in the black leather chair behind Swallow's desk and had barely gotten settled when the door he had just closed was slowly opened by Little Paulie. On his return from the men's room, he had seen Price enter the office and thought it was probably the person he meant to kill.

"Who the hell are you?" Paulie demanded when he realized the man he faced was much older than the man he sought. He had drawn his .45 and leveled it at Price, who realized he had blundered into an untenable situation.

"Nobody you know," was his response and were the words he thought might be the last ones he was likely to utter. He knew something of Paulie's type and figured correctly the man was not only bent on murder but would surely dispose of any incidental witnesses.

"Cut the crap," Paulie said. "Who are you?"

"I'm Bill Price, a retired detective with the city police department," he replied, aware nothing he said would make any difference and there was no reason not to tell the truth.

"You're a cop?"

"I was a cop," Price replied and went on to explain the police get just as upset when retirees are shot as they do when it happens to officers on active duty. "They don't make any distinction between the two," he added, stalling for time.

"Me neither," Paulie, who meant to pull the trigger, said an instant before his body went rigid and both eyes bulged in response to a fatal trauma that had been inflicted on him. Price watched incredulously as the blade of a knife emerged from Paulie's throat followed by gushing blood, red and messy as it spilled onto the light gray carpeting at his feet. The dying man stood there briefly and then slumped dead to the floor, his gun falling harmlessly with him.

"Jesus," Price exclaimed as he realized Aldo Carnavali had silently entered the office and plunged a long, slender blade into the back of Paulie's neck with such force it came out the front. "Where did you

144

come from?" he asked, although he quickly understood that Aldo's entry into the room had been blocked from his view by Paulie, who stood between them.

"I saw him follow you into the office," Aldo explained, his manner surprisingly calm for the considerable effort he had just made. "I got the knife from the kitchen when I thought there might be trouble."

"I guess I owe you my life," Price observed, rising from the chair.

"I guess you do," Aldo conceded without a trace of the Italian accent he used so liberally in the dining room.

Chapter Sixteen

"I think she broke my heart," McCurdy said to Price as they sat at The Bristol's bar where they had been since lunch much earlier.

"You don't have a heart ," Price replied, "and not much of a liver, either." McCurdy, who had finished four drinks to his friend's two, had just disclosed his short affair with Mimi Swallow and admitted she had dumped him for someone else. He had figured out there was another man, but didn't know it was her gynecologist. That revelation would not have lessened McCurdy's sense of loss but would surely have amused Price.

McCurdy had not intended to tell Price or anyone else about his brief relationship with the younger woman, but the collision of his depressed thoughts about her and four stiff drinks loosened his thoughts and his tongue as well. "I really miss her," he said, fiddling with one of the four swizzle sticks that had been served with his drinks. "I really do."

"Yeah," Price observed, "and I really miss the time before you told me about the whole mess. It now seems like a golden age." The sarcasm was lost on McCurdy, who motioned the bartender, Willie Sutton Sikes, for still another drink. "If you're going to get sloshed, I'm going home," Price added.

"Nope," McCurdy said with some resolve. "This is the last one and I'm going to sip it to death."

Price looked at the man he had known since their rooky years on the police force and tried to imagine what he had looked like in those days. The image of a youthful McCurdy, however, was overwhelmed by the present reality and Price's imagination could only come up with the same old face and a head of darker hair. "Where did it go?" he thought in reference to his life, but said aloud: "I've got something to tell you." He wondered if McCurdy was sober enough to understand what he was about to be told.

"Huh?" was the response, which didn't inspire Price with confidence his friend was in any condition to handle serious conversation. But he felt time was running short and decided to say what he thought needed to be said. "I've got inoperable cancer," he told McCurdy, who at first didn't seem to absorb the information, but turned to him a few moments later and inquired: "What kind?"

"It doesn't matter," Price replied. "They all have the same eventual result." He went on to ask McCurdy to dispose of his physical possessions and make certain the various models of Nelson's flagship, Victory, were carefully shipped to a small naval historical museum specified in his will. "You can have anything else in the apartment," Price said.

"I don't need another cheap blue suit," McCurdy replied, thinking somewhat later that Price would probably need it for his funeral and unaware there would be no formal burial for a man who insisted on cremation and the distribution of his ashes to the four winds. Price told McCurdy that Andrew Masterson – who had left the country for an undisclosed tropical destination but who had agreed to shuttle back to the city – would administer his will.

"I'd ask you to administer the estate, but you couldn't administer your butt with outside help," he said. He revealed to McCurdy the bulk of his estate would go to several charitable organizations in the city, but said nothing about the $50,000 that had been designated for his friend. He assumed McCurdy would probably squander the money in short order, but that possibility seemed consistent to Price with the nature of a true gift.

"How much time to you have?" McCurdy asked, not offended by

Price's evaluation of his administrative skills. He knew he was a lousy manager, and wasn't bothered by that particular shortcoming.

"Who knows?"

McCurdy made some observation about the inaccuracy of longevity estimates made by medical professionals, aware the cliché was not likely to make any difference to Price but doing it mainly because he could think of little else to say. Finally, he looked at his old friend, noticing for the first time the dark coloration under his eyes, and shook his head. "Well, crap," he said and they changed the subject.

Back east, word of Little Paulie's death reached his mob boss, Zeno Magruder, who also learned about the circumstances that led to the killing. Originally angered by Paulie's rash indifference to the organization's chain of command, he came to realize that a restaurant waiter had done what he otherwise would have had to have done. Aldo Carnavali had accomplished legally what Magruder would have had to do criminally, and the act had saved him the cost of a contract on Paulie's life. Once he realized things had worked out to his satisfaction, he anonymously sent a case of good Chianti to Aldo, who was mystified by the unexpected gift but, never-the-less, shared it with Grace Goodson over the following weeks. Aldo was not a man to look a gift horse in the mouth.

Another mob boss, Dom Chino, was less gratified by a turn of events that had transformed two of his underlings, Ivor McCusky and Big Al Moroski, into corpses, both on the same day. The job had been done, he knew, by a relative newcomer to the gang, known to him as Andy Anderson but, in reality, FBI agent Andy Masterson, who McCusky had targeted as a possible mole. The target, Chino realized, had turned the situation around, shot his would-be killers to death and disappeared. And even worse from his point of view, the resources of a substantial criminal network were unable to find a trace of the fugitive, who had no need to find underworld refuge where Chino's connections would have been the most effective in seeking him out. Eventually, the pressures of other illegal business diverted the gangster's attention from the search, and Masterson was left to cautiously pursue a new life.

Earlier on the day Price told McCurdy about his cancer, he phoned

Desmond Black and disclosed that a previously unsuspected woman, Mona Swallow, had arranged the killing of the killer, Dandy Frank Baines. With his usual reserve, Black accepted the information about the man who had brutally murdered his daughter and only child, and thanked Price for his effort. Inwardly, however, the news was a bitter disappointment based mainly on his own failure to dispatch Baines. He had put out a contract on the killer's life that would have given him greater satisfaction had it been successful. Although a wealthy and respected member of the community in which his family had long functioned among its top ranks, Desmond Black had all the instincts of the mob boss he had employed through indirect channels to kill the man who killed his daughter. The failure of this effort would haunt him to the end of his days.

Price had no way of knowing about Black's regret, and had called him out of sympathy for a man who had lost his child to a detestable thug who fully deserved what could easily be described as a predictable fate. In all probability, Price would have understood Black's feelings, although he would have wondered why he hadn't taken matters into his own hands and either shot, stabbed or otherwise rendered the miscreant dead. Despite his years as a so-called officer of the law, he saw the legal system as a cumbersome machine that sometimes intruded itself on real justice.

In what Price considered a final irony, a note was found on Little Paulie's body that carried the name of a long-dead Frenchman, Pierre Charles Jean Baptiste Silvestre de Villeneuve. Hagle had been puzzled by the discovery, which remained a minor mystery until he mentioned it to Price and learned the man was the admiral who commanded Napoleon's fleet at the battle of Trafalgar. His defeat and disgrace was ultimately Napoleon's fault but was carried out by the English ships under the command of Nelson, whose flagship, Victory, had been replicated in Price's models.

Neither Price nor Hagle knew, or would ever know, that the note among Paulie's personal possessions was simply a reminder to canvas some library for a biography of the French admiral. Paulie revered Napoleon much as Price held Nelson in esteem, and had often sought

150

out reading material on related personalities. His death had spared him knowledge of Villeneuve's crushing defeat which, like the battle of Waterloo, he would have taken as a personal tragedy.

"Is there anything I can do?" McCurdy inquired of Price after a long silence. The two men had lingered at the bar for no particular reason a long time after the check had been paid and the bartender, Sikes, had removed their empty glasses.

"About what?" Price replied.

"About the god-damn cancer," McCurdy explained and went on to offer his services in the variety of ways care givers seek to ease the inconveniences inflicted on the sick. He offered to drive him to various medical appointments, run errands and anything else that needed to be done as his friend endured what he believed was the inevitable struggle ahead.

"I appreciate your concern, but I'm okay," Price said with insufficient conviction to convince his friend, who understood any further pursuit of the matter would serve no practical purpose. Instead, he decided to go home and explained that intention to Price as he stiffly dismounted the bar stool and stood erect. "I'll call you tomorrow," were his final words as he strolled off toward the main entrance with the intention of fetching his car.

"He's probably not in any condition to drive," Price, still seated at the bar, thought, but knew there was no point in trying to persuade McCurdy to take a taxi. Despite a long police career that should have taught him otherwise, he was one of those drinkers who never doubted his ability to drive under the influence of alcohol or anything else. And, Price admitted to himself, McCurdy had never so much as dented a car or injured himself or anyone else.

Forty-five minutes later, McCurdy arrived home safely and Price was still seated at the bar where Floyd Sparrow found him deep in thought and not yet ready to leave the restaurant. "We can't get that bastard's blood out of the carpet in my office," Floyd said without real annoyance and fully aware he was lucky to be alive. Little Paulie, he had learned, made two attempts on his life and failed both times.

"I'd leave it there as a reminder Aldo deserves a raise," Price

151

suggested. They then commenced a long, rambling conversation in which Sparrow told the old man about his intention to take his dead brother's two children, along with his own son and daughter, on a western vacation, and other plans to fill the paternal void in their young lives. He said he planned to marry June Havens, although not until an appropriate amount of time had elapsed since the death of his wife, Mona. "I don't really give a damn," Floyd explained, "but June thinks it's the only decent thing to do." And he thanked Price for everything he had done during a dangerous and trying period in his life.

"It's nothing compared to what The Bristol has meant to me," Price told him plainly but with a good deal of nostalgia for a place that had been the setting for some of the best moments in his own life. It was thoughts of those times that made him linger at the bar after McCurdy's departure. As he sat there alone, a series of tableaus streamed through his mind, all but obliterating the real world that went on, quietly for a change, around him. He thought mainly of Diana Hornbeck, who had occupied with him at one time or another every bar stool down that long and splendidly maintained hardwood counter. He had been able to recapture the sound of her voice, which had lately escaped him, and her scent which had been, he knew, the essence of some cologne rather than something fundamental to her person.

Price recalled an evening many years earlier when Diana, repulsed by some drunk's vulgar language, had gotten off her barstool, drink in hand, and walked the few steps to a nearby table where the offender sat with two other men. "Watch your fucking language," she told him just before she dashed her drink, ice cubes and all, into his florid face. Price also remembered that the man, momentarily stupefied, eventually rose, probably with the intention of extracting some form of revenge for the surprise attack. Had his friends not restrained him and had not Price fetched her back to the bar, the drunk surely would have broken her pretty nose or done some other damage, Price reminisced.

On another night in the misty past, he and McCurdy rescued an attractive woman from an abusive companion who had slapped her sharply across the face and doubled his fist to strike another and more forceful blow. "Not tonight," Price told him as his own fist collided with the man's jaw, dropping him instantly to the floor while McCurdy escorted the woman away from the conflict. Price subsequently dragged the abuser to his feet, identified himself as an off-duty police detective, and warned him of the consequences if he ever bothered the woman again. McCurdy, meanwhile, drove her home and established a relationship that lasted for the next six months.

And it was at the bar in The Bristol that Diana revealed to Price the affliction that would claim her life. He had originally thought the disease an inconvenience they had to endure, but one that would eventually pass and leave them more or less as they had been. Her subsequent death taught him that all obstacles are not surmountable, something he should have known before but a reality that had eluded his notice.

"I don't intend to be punched, poked or prodded in some germ-ridden hospital," she had told him as they sat at The Bristol bar together for the last time. She meant she had no intention of submission to a course of treatment that was painful, demeaning and had only a scant chance of success. She had thoroughly researched her condition and prospects, discussed it at length with her doctors and come to terms with the notion of an early death, a concept Price found more difficult to accept until he realized it was her decision to make. "Okay, honey," he had said to her at last, "it's your call."

Now, faced with a situation that was similar in some respects, Price understood to a deeper extent the reasoning that had motivated Diana. He also understood the main difference in their circumstances was age. She had been confronted with the dilemma as a relatively young woman and he, on the other hand, had lived a full life. Given the dangerous nature of his work, he had not, in fact, expected to live as long as he had.

Like Diana, Price had no inclination to die, either pain or drug-ridden, in some remote corner of a large, impersonal hospital. He had invited death at the hands of Little Paulie by holstering his gun after he entered Floyd Swallow's office and would surely have died there had Aldo Carnavali not influenced those events. He had also considered and rejected the use of his service revolver in a suicide he knew would

153

void large insurance policies whose proceeds were meant to support several local charities and medical research into the disease that killed Diana. That would be a waste, he figured, just as scattering bits of his brain about the apartment would be too reminiscent of the lethal untidiness he had witnessed so often in his long police career.

These were the thoughts that occupied Price as he left The Bristol that night to discover a misty rain and light fog had cooled the air and impaired visibility somewhat. Self absorbed and headed for his car, he stepped off the curb in front of the restaurant and was struck and instantly killed by a speeding medical emergency truck whose flashing lights had been obscured from him by nearby parked cars. Or that was the conclusion reached by those who investigated the accident.

Jack McCurdy – whose wife, Missy, was asleep in her separate bedroom when he came home – had gone to the kitchen where he scrambled two eggs, made toast and hungrily ate the surrogate breakfast before he went off to bed. He had laid awake for some time and was still half conscious when the phone on his nightstand jangled him out of his stupor. "Yeah," he said with some effort when he had fumbled the instrument to a useful position.

"Bill Price is dead," the voice on the other end of the line announced. It was Floyd Sparrow, who went on to identify himself and explain he didn't know who else to call. He told McCurdy about the accident, omitting the fact that Price had been struck with such great force his body was all but unrecognizable. "I was just talking to him not 15 minutes before the accident," he added.

"Accident, my ass," McCurdy thought, recalling Price's revelation about the cancer and his own conviction his friend had sought immediate relief from his ailment in preference to a lingering and probably painful death. But he thanked Swallow for his consideration and began the long process of missing his old friend.

THE END

154

Other Books by Dave Snyder

Mexican Summer and Other Seasons

A memoir centered in Mexico during the summer of 1950 that recalls earlier events, both personal and historical.

French Spring and its Aftermath

Still another memoir, this one commencing with a trip to Europe aboard the original Queen Mary in 1951 and continuing through most of the author's life.

The Murderous Dilemma of Bill Price

The introduction of the fictional detective, Bill Price, and the first volume in The Bill Price Trilogy.

The Deadly Transit of Toby Barnes

The second volume in The Trilogy and the one in which Bill Price tracks his principal adversary.

The books were published by Kleenan Press and are available for $8.95 each from the publisher. The address is: P.O. Box 1213; Walled Lake, Michigan 48390.